DOUBLE TRIANGLES

Jeanette C. Pope

To Mary,
Good Reading
Jeanette C Pope

ROYAL MEDIA
AND PUBLISHING LLC

Royal Media and Publishing
P. O. Box 4321
Jeffersonville, IN 47131
502-802-5385
http://www.royalmediaandpublishing.com

Cover Design: Bill Lacy

ISBN-10: 0-9987154-1-7
ISBN-13: 978-0-9987154-1-4

Printed in the United States of America

Dedication

In the memory of, Valerie Mansfield. May you continue to rest in heaven. I love you and miss you.

Acknowledgements

I give all honor to God for without His grace the creation of this novel could not be possible. Thank You, Lord, for the vision and favor You've shown me.

I would also like to express my sincerest appreciation to my husband, Lawrence A. Pope, Sr. who has supported me in everything that I have achieved throughout my life.

A special thank you to my children, Terri Pope-Carr and Lawrence A. Pope, Jr. for having confidence in my writing abilities.

Many thanks to Peggy Lewis for the encouragement to not only write this book but to step out on faith and get it published.

Finally, I would like to thank Rev. Dr. Kevin Cosby for steering me in the direction of my amazing publisher, Julia Royston. She has held my hand all the way to the end. Thank you, Julia!

TABLE of CONTENTS

Introduction

Spring season is the time for celebrations in Louisville, Kentucky. The city is filled with excitement and anticipation of the world famous Kentucky Derby.

However, the city's Derby activities will be lost on Danielle Johnston, who is returning to Louisville to bury her 23-year-old-sister. But the grief of her sister's death is only the beginning of many unresolved problems she will face during her brief stay in her hometown.

One of the unavoidable problems she will face is the handsome Kevin Williams, who will try to convince Danielle to rekindle their love affair.

But there is also a deadly ghost, waiting for Danielle's return. This evil spirit wants to end her life.

DOUBLE
TRIANGLES

CHAPTER ONE

The Boeing 747 plane was descending, a mind-voice alerted Danielle. The mind-voice and fog had been entering her subconscious being ever since she'd received the phone call that changed her life forever. She could not process the news that the caller reported, so she had been functioning on human autopilot. This fog covered her mind protectively whenever reality started to make her face the darkness that lay before her. She smiled at a small comparison of her mind to an autopilot. What she had to face when this plane landed caused her to look out of the plane's window and think that if the aircraft smashed into the runway and killed only her then that would be just fine. Thinking too much caused the real world to start to creep into her brain, and Danielle wasn't ready to face it, so mercifully the mind fog set in again, then she had no other thoughts. Minutes later the little voice told her that is time to leave the plane.

Removing her large sunglasses Danielle checked her makeup and assured that everything was still the same. As she studied her beautiful, smooth, dark chocolate face, she checked off her personal beauty list. Her skin was dark chocolate, and smooth as silk, her lips were full with just the right shade of pink, and her hair was long, ebony, shiny and straight, but her eyes were puffy and red. Closing the compact, she concluded that there was nothing to be done about the red eyes for they may be red forever.

She felt content with covering her eyes with sunglasses to avoid the stares from the public. To keep up appearances, Danielle had purposely worn tight fitting white Capris and a navy blue shirt that stopped right at the top of her pants. Together they showed off her shapely body, and the colors enhanced her skin tone. The purpose of the slightly short shirt was just to give the men a small teaser; a look at her flat tummy as she reached up or twisted in a certain way. The navy blue heels she wore gave her body a great sway to her already suggestive walk. One might be in bereavement, but one shouldn't look bereaved. That was her reasoning.

As she walked through the airport with the sway of a runway model, the stares of appreciation from old and young men were completely lost on her because she could only feel the numbing fog in her brain.

Giving her shirt a tug, she couldn't remember how long she had been standing in the luggage department. She became aware that she was losing track of how many times the bags had gone around. This time, she would try harder to focus on recognizing her luggage. Looking around the Standiford Field Airport, her mind wondered again. How ironic it was to be back here again. She had left Louisville, Kentucky in tears from a life changing experience only to return four years later in tears from another life changing experience. This time, she really couldn't see herself surviving this tragedy.

My 23-year-old sister is dead! My only family member is dead! Her mind screamed. The thoughts had overcome the protective fog and sliced through her brain causing her to give a small moan but mercifully, the fog returned to numb her brain, therefore, freezing every thought. Once again in her coma-like state, she tried to focus on finding her luggage.

Lieutenant Kevin Williams was in the airport as well. He hated to blend in with the rest of the men admiring Danielle's beauty. She looked great, as always. He hadn't seen her in four years. In fact, the last time he saw her she had threatened to bodily harm him if he ever approached her again. She had made it very clear that she wanted nothing more to do with him, and she had good cause. Even though he could see the devastating grief on her face, he could also see the hate and hurt in her eyes whenever she removed the large, dark sunglasses to wipe away her tears.

But today, he would just have to take a chance that she wouldn't kill him in the airport. What a coward, he thought of himself. She only weighed 110 pounds, but her temper would make King Kong shiver. She was the most stubborn woman he'd ever met. In her world, everything existed in black or white or good or bad. There was never a middle ground or gray area in the world that she had built for herself. Somehow she was going to listen to him; her life may depend on it but yet there he stood in the airport dreading the head-on collision, and that was putting it mildly.

The killer was also in the airport hiding among the array of public telephone stands. This person was enjoying the agony on Danielle's face. "She's still trying to be pretty." The person whispered with mocking pity. "But it ain't working you slut! You sinful bitch! I can't wait till I slide my blade into your pretty little neck. I will take my time with you. It won't be like the game I played with Samantha. "Please, please don't hurt me!" she begged. "I made her think I wasn't going to kill her. Dumb bitch! But I will not play games with you... Sin should be wiped out!"

A passer-by looked around when the whispering got louder. The Person ducked back behind the Welcome to Louisville sign. *"Oh!"* The Person whispered softly. Seeing Kevin sent The Person into a rage. *"What the hell is he doing here? They should not be together. They couldn't wait?! He had to come to the airport! She's a whore, and she will die soon!" The person raged on in a hushed voice. But the whispers were getting louder, causing a man using a nearby public pay phone to look in The Person's direction. The Person looked around as well so the man couldn't identify them. While turning around, The Person saw a police officer coming near the welcome sign. "I must go. The World Trade Center bombing last year makes it hard for a citizen to do business."* Giving Danielle and Kevin a final look, The Person scurried away from the welcome area and proceeded out of the airport.

Danielle's brain fog alerted her that someone was calling her name. As she turned toward the sound, her mind started to scream, "Nooo! Not now!"

"Danny, are you alright?" She looked up to see a 6"3 African America man, Lieutenant Kevin Williams, the last man on earth that she wanted to see. It also shocked her to realize that he still looked very appealing to her. Instantly, she remembered how his caramel brown skin felt against hers. Suddenly she wanted to touch his short curly black hair. With his hands in his pockets, his confident, sexy stand almost made her forget how much she hated him. *Almost.* Then she remembered that their love could never be again and the reason why. The memories of their last encounter quickly returned filling her heart with a murderous rage. Looking straight into his dangerously dark eyes, she hissed, "What the hell are you doing here?"

"I came to help." He said lamely.

"I don't need any help. Just stay away from me."

"You do need help, Danny." Kevin replied, "I've watched you for ten minutes trying to claim your bag. How is that working for you?"

"Go away! You must. I can't deal with you right now!" She urgently pleaded.

Stepping closer to her, Kevin said, "I have y---"

He was cut off by a police officer, "Ma'am is there a problem here?" The officer, who was 5'9 looked to be of solid muscle and in good physical shape. Even though he had a no non–sense approach, the flash of his white teeth let Kevin know that the officer had more than saving Danielle on his mind. Kevin became angrier as he watched Danielle respond to the officer's manliness. Kevin looked at the name plate on the broad chest of this officer to find that his name was Gaines.

Flashing his LPD shield, Kevin said, "This is a private matter. Move on!"

Looking at Kevin's badge, then back at Danielle, Officer Gaines asked, "Will you be okay if I leave you with him?" Kevin's eyes never left the officer. Fog or no fog Danielle could see that this situation was going to escalate shortly.

"No, I will be fine. I'm ok." She said smiling sweetly. The extra sweet smile was meant to stick it to Kevin.

"Are you sure? All you have to do is say the word." Officer Gaines said, looking directly at Kevin.

That was the last straw for Kevin, who stepped into the officer's space and hissed in a low threatening voice, "Step off. The lady told you that she's ok. If you don't leave, I will see that you are reassigned to protect the dog pound. Understand?"

Trying to maintain some shred of cockiness, the officer once again asked Danielle, "So, no problem here?"

"No. Everything is fine." She replied.

When Gaines slowly walked away, Kevin again turned his attention to Danielle.

"We need to talk. I already have your bags."

"You didn't have to do that. I can take care of myself."

Kevin started to tell her how he had picked up her luggage in front of her some time ago, but that would only lead to a huge fight so, he would take the low road.

"I know you can take care of yourself. I need to talk to you about Sam." He said softly and sincerely.

"What about Sam?" Danielle questioned suspiciously.

"We can't talk here." Picking up her designer bags, he started to walk.

Following him, Danielle asked, "Where are we going?"

Turning to leave he said, "We are going to Lauren's house. She is waiting."

"Wait, damn it! What the hell is going on?! You just can't show up here and start telling me what to do. Put the bags down and start talking!" She demanded.

Now everyone in the airport was looking, and Officer Gaines was returning quickly.

Kevin knew he had to get a quick hold on the scene because it was getting out of hand quickly.

Stepping close to Danielle he said between clenched teeth. "Danny, if you don't come with me, I will arrest you and make you do the whole 72 hours of insanity observations, is that clear?! You better make Officer Gaines think that this is a misunderstanding!"

Seeing how serious, threatening, and dangerous Kevin looked, Danielle quickly turned to Officer Gaines and flashed a sexy smile, "I am sorry we keep causing a situation here, but my brother can sometimes be so bossy. Mom sent him," she lied.

"Oh," the officer said seeming to understand.

Stepping close to him she said, "I will be here for a couple of days, can I call you?"

The man nearly fainted, and he fumbled with his business card. "Sure! Call me anytime. I will be glad to show you the town. What is your name?" he asked with a grin that covered his face.

"I am Danielle Johnston, but you can call me Danny." Taking his card she swooned, "I'll be calling you soon."

Turning to Kevin, who was steaming, she said, "Come on, *big brother,* let's go home."

To Gaines, she waved, "Bye, now."

Kevin picked up the bags and walked to the exit with Danielle strolling behind him. He knew this would not be easy and getting her to go with him wasn't even the hardest part. He had won that battle slightly bruised, by the *big brother* comment. They would have to walk to his car because he did not trust this woman, if he left her for one minute, she would bolt. Tugging her luggage, he walked to his personal car, a shiny black on black 1994 Lincoln Continental. Danielle just stood there brooding as he struggled to put the bags into the trunk of the big car; it wasn't that the trunk wasn't big enough, it was just how much was packed into them.

After the bags had been loaded, he went to the passenger side of the Lincoln to open the door for her. She gave him a dirty look that he could see through her glasses as she slid into the roomy car.

The Lincoln rolled smoothly out of the airport's parking lot and onto the highway. Soon the nose of the car was headed toward the West end of Louisville, Danielle asked, "Where are we going?"

Another fight was about to begin Kevin thought, but what could he do? It couldn't be avoided, but this time he knew he could keep control of the battle. He had a weapon this time. He would pull from the sisterhood friendship Danny used to share with his sister and the guilt that she must feel for abandoning the relationship.

As he concentrated on the road he casually answered, "To Lauren's house. She demanded that I bring you straight to her house."

Smiling she said, "Aww, that's sweet of her, but I have made reservations at the Seelbach Hotel downtown."

"Let's just go see her before you check in," Kevin suggested mildly.

"No, this isn't social hour, Kevin. I've got to go to Sam's apartment to find insurance papers and to make funeral arrangements. I'd rather do this by myself."

Pulling the car off the highway to the shoulder of the road, Kevin said, "We need to talk."

He looked so serious that Danielle didn't even shoot a smart-ass response. Turning to face him she asked. "What?"

Reaching for her hand, he said, "Danny, Sam was murdered."

"What?! No, they told me she had an accident!" She screamed, pulling her hand back. The fog did not come this time. The numbness didn't come for her either, and she felt every pain of his words. She snatched her hand from him, and began screaming, "No! No! This can't be true!"

"I sorry, Danny!" Kevin said with his heart breaking for her loss.

Danielle removed the large designer sunglasses, buried her face in her hand and began to sob.

When Kevin reached for her, she violently pulled away. "Don't," she managed to say through the heartbreaking sobs, "Leave me alone."

Now it was time, Kevin thought. Let round two of the fight start. It was time for some truths.

"Why, Danny? What, once again you can do everything by yourself?" He paused, she didn't answer. "Well, you can't. This is too big for you."

"How was she murdered?"

"Baby, I'm sorry to tell you this but she was stabbed three times in the chest area. We think it was a break in." Kevin said softly. He was hurting too. He also was close to Sam.

Danielle was hysterical now; she bent over putting her face into her lap.

Kevin couldn't bear to see her suffer like this and not be able to comfort her in some way so, he reached for her again. "Come here, baby."

"Just leave me alone, Kevin!" Danny replied through slobs.

"You are alone, baby. You know that the only person that can get you through this is me. No matter how much you hate me, at this moment you need me, and only me. Let me help you."

This time, she didn't resist when he pulled her into his arms where she cried for at least 15 minutes.

She had not been in his arms in over four years, but yet it felt like she was just there yesterday. The love she felt for him was beginning to make itself known to her senses and her body. She could feel him kissing her face, and the urge got stronger for her to feel his lips once again so, she turned her face toward his and they shared a longing kiss.

As they pulled apart from the embrace, Kevin said, "I love you, Danny. I've never stopped loving you."

He felt her body stiffen then she abruptly withdrew from his arms.

With icicles hanging on each word she said, "You have no right to love me, Kevin. What would your wife have to say about your love for me?"

Feeling the air in the car turn from passionate heat to frostbiting cold, Kevin said, "Okay, Let's go to Lauren's."

"Okay," Danielle whispered as she snapped the seat belt around her body. Replacing the large sunglasses, she leaned back and let her friends the fog and the numbness take over. She just stared ahead as the big car merged into the heavy traffic on the Watterson Highway.

The weather was typical for spring in Kentucky. It could change from cold to warm or from rain to snow all in one day. Kevin loved this time of year because the city seemed to be buzzing with the anticipation of the Derby festivities to come but there in the bible-belt of the world, Easter was on the minds of the Christians and retailers as well.

Spring in the bluegrass state always shouted the promise of new hope for the future, at least it seemed that way to Kevin as he eased the big car through the streets of downtown Louisville. He passed the Masonic Hall, the place that was supposed to be their first date. A smile crossed his face as he remembered his sister Lauren begging him to take Danny to the Annual Spring Fling Thing, a dance that was being held there back in April of 1989.

Lauren and Danny had met in grade school and became best friends. Kevin who was three years older never paid any attention to the girls and their drama with their other friends. After begging, bargaining and threatening, he had given into Lauren and agreed to be Danny's date for the dance. It didn't hurt that Danny's uncle and guardian were sponsoring the function, and it also didn't hurt that Danny's uncle was a

Captain in the Louisville Police Department because Kevin was in officer training. On the other hand, he knew that this girl must be handled with kid gloves because everyone knew how protective the Captain and Mrs. Johnston were of Danielle and Samantha, her younger sister.

But when he asked her to go to the dance with him, she looked at him with suspicion and asked, "Did Lauren make you ask me to the Spring Fling?" With a quick response, he said, "No, girl. Look, I have been busy, and the dance slipped up on me, this year. Now, I need a baby cakes on my arm, and you fit the bill."

Her eyes became narrow, and she hissed the words, "Baby cakes?! Are you serious?"

At that moment he realized that this girl was *pepper,* a word used by older African-American men when they referenced an ill-tempered woman.

"I assure you that I do *not* want to be your baby cakes for tonight, I could get a date if I wanted one. Now leave, I have studying to do." She responded sounding irritated.

At that point, he became interested. He couldn't believe that she would rather study than attend a party given by her aunt and uncle on a Saturday night!

"What are you studying? Maybe I can help."

"Go away, Kevin. I have work to do," she repeated.

"No really, I want to help. What can I do?"

"Okay. If you are pulling my chain, you will pay dearly." She warned. Then she paused and gave him an evaluative look. Satisfied that he may be serious, she said, "The first thing you need to do is to read my notes and highlight the important parts, then make note cards. I will make an assessment from my notes and then you can quiz me. Still want to stay and help?"

"If I do this, I will make the assessment because you will choose only things that are your strength. If you are serious then you should review your strengths and study your weaknesses." After a pause, he asked, "Is this a challenge?"

"Maybe," she answered.

"Then, I accept," he said. Pulling off his windbreaker, he was ready to take on the task. By looking at Danny's face, he could see that she was serious about studying and since he'd pushed the issue of helping, he was in for the long haul.

"So, this means that you will go to the dance with me when we finish?"

"If you make it through this study session, I will go to the dance with you."

They worked well together as they dug into statistics, terms, definitions and examples. The harmony of it came while making sense of the information, studying the note cards as well as making and taking Kevin's created assessment. They graded and analyzed the exam and determined that the study session was a success. However, now it was too late to go to the party.

"Kevin, look at the time. It is too late to go to the dance. I am so sorry; sometimes I get so wrapped up in my work that I totally forget time."

"Okay, so now you get to do what I want to do since I missed my party. Let's go to the Screaming Eagles."

The Screaming Eagles Club was a famous motorcycle club, and it was very popular at Kentucky Derby time. Up and down the neighborhood, vendors set up stations to sell everything from food to clothing. Most people went to the area to enjoy the festive atmosphere as well as the best barbecue, ribs, and chicken in the city. Besides the vendors there were also blocks of music, partying and dancing.

"Unc told me never to go there, besides we won't get in the clubhouse since it's so close to Derby."

"Well, he is right, you shouldn't go there by yourself, but you will be with the police. How much safer can you be?"

She laughed and said, "Police want-to-be!"

"We are the best kind because we try harder. Let's go." He said laughing.

They went to the Screaming Eagles but just as they predicted, the little place was so crowded that they couldn't get inside so, they walked around the crowded streets and visited most of the vendors.

The music in the streets was great and added to the festive celebration. Kevin was surprised to see that not only was Danny having a good time, but she was a fantastic dancer.

They danced so much that they didn't realize how much time had passed until they both noticed the light in the sky. He smiled remembering the panic swelling in their hearts as they ran to the car, wishing that they could turn back the time. Both of them had a sense of dread knowing they'd have to face an angry Captain Johnston. In spite of the pending doom, as soon as he opened the car door, Danny kissed him and it was not a "let's just be friends" kiss. The kiss promised that more would be coming. However, it was four o'clock in the morning and he had to take her home. Kevin opened up the glove compartment of the 1989 Lincoln and took out his cell phone to call Captain Johnston. Needless to say, the conversation did not go well. As predicted, the Captain was not pleased with Kevin for keeping his niece from attending the dance and for taking her into what he considered to be a dangerous environment.

The memory of their first kiss was still on his mind when he pulled into his sister's driveway. He turned the car motor off and sat there for a moment dreading the conversation they were about to have once inside the house. But so far he'd won most of the battles, so maybe with his sister's help, he could just possibly win the war.

CHAPTER TWO

Danny opened her eyes when the car stopped moving. There in front of her was a sense of peace. The ranch style house, with dark gray shutters and dark gray trim stood in front of her and filled her fragile mind with excitement. She could feel the love oozing from the gray stones of the house. Lauren and her husband Anthony were loving people and loyal friends. What made this lovesome situation uncomfortable for her was they loved Kevin as well.

Her eyes wandered over to the flowers in the front yard planted by her and Lauren four years ago. The yard was immaculate. There wasn't a blade of grass, nor a leaf in any bush that was out of place. They had bought this house together before they got married. She wished she could have come home for their wedding, but it would have been too painful.

 Hearing a car door slam, Lauren's husband of four years came to join her at the large picture window. Anthony was about as tall as Kevin, but he was very muscular, and he worked out every day to stay that way. While Kevin stayed active working out at the gym and playing basketball, Anthony was serious about staying buff. He kept his head shaved to keep from stressing about his hair falling out. Half of a head of hair just wasn't his style. Touching the hair around his mouth and chin reassured him that he had made the right choice by growing hair on his face and not on his head. He thought that the hair on his face and his golden brown skin complemented him well or at least his wife agreed.

Peering through the window and slightly concealed by the thin off white curtains, he observed that his wife's best friend looked thoroughly pissed, and that his partner and brother-in-law looked very uncomfortable. It amused Anthony to see Kevin so irritated because he was always so cold, dark, and unemotional about everything and everyone except Danny. Anthony's lips curved into a devilish smile as he thought, 'that girl will be his undoing.'

Leaving Lauren at the window, Anthony went through the side door of the house to the driveway to help with the luggage but mainly to find out what happened at the airport.

Lauren hugged Danny tightly as she came through the door. Lauren was a nurse practitioner and was always concerned about health issues for family and friends. Looking at her friend, Danny could see that Lauren hadn't changed at all during their four years apart. Her coco brown skin was as flawless as ever, and Danny could barely see the scar on her forehead just below her hairline. It surprised

Danny that Lauren was wearing her thick long black hair away from her face because immediately after the car accident she had used her hair to cover the scar on her forehead. Danny tried over and over to reassure her that the injury didn't take away from her beauty, but Lauren was not convinced.

Coming into the living room, Danny was amazed at the progress Lauren and Anthony had made decorating and furnishing the house. The living room felt comfy and soothing with the oversized couch and chairs. For Lauren to be so tiny, the furniture she picked was just the opposite.

Danny was surprised to see Teah sitting in one of the overstuffed chairs. Although there were four friends in their group, Lindsey and Teah were close, but Lauren and Danny were closer. Teah wasn't as attractive as the other girls in the group, but she didn't seem to mind and because of her low self-esteem, the other girls always protected her. Lauren and Lindsey helped her to dress to enhance her appearance. From an early age, the group of friends realized that she would have big breasts, so it was a struggle for the girls to keep them supported and covered.

Looking at her now, Danny concluded that they had lost the battle. Since Teah was short, Danny always thought that one day those bosoms would topple her over. Danny and

Sam had helped Teah to read and write; they worked with her every day after school. Teah would often get angry at them because it was so hard for her to comprehend what they were teaching her. In the end, Danny always soothed away her apprehensions and insisted she continue to learn what they were teaching her each day.

Standing there looking at her friend in the ill-fitting outfit, she wondered if she put the learning to work for her and got a job.

"Teah!" Danny exclaimed feeling glad to see her. "I am happy to see you,"

Standing Teah said, "I'm so sorry to hear about Sam." As Teah hugged Danny, she saw Kevin and Anthony talking at the back of the Lincoln. "Wow! You work fast, girl! You just got here and already hooked up with Kevin?!" Sarcastically she added, "You *do* know he is married now."

Danny stepped back from her embrace ready to reply, but Lauren interrupted.

"No," she said firmly, "This is not about to happen. She just lost her sister and I will not let anything more hurtful happen to her."

"Me? I'm not hurting her. Your brother is…" Teah replied. "I just don't want her to get wrapped up in him again because you know and I know he will never leave Lindsey."

"That is not our concern. Our concern is to support our friend as she prepares to bury her sister." Lauren said walking very close to Teah. "Not another word about Lindsey. Not one word."

The words "bury her sister" made Danny break down and cry. The situation was getting real, and she just wasn't ready to face burying Sam. She sat on the overstuffed couch, covered her face with her hands and cried. Lauren and Teah went to her and rubbed her back while she cried.

Anthony could hear Danny crying, which was rare, she was a very strong young lady. He knew that if anything could make her cry it would be Sam's death or his best friend, Kevin. This situation was breaking his heart, too. He prayed that Kevin and Danny would work out their problems. Looking at his friend, he knew that they would never stop loving each other. He just hoped that they would find the path back to each other.

"I see you won the battle of getting her here. Which ball did you lose?" Anthony laughed.

"Man, that's not funny! That is the most infuriating woman on earth!"

"The hell it ain't. Watching Mr. Cool defrost at a rapid rate, it's priceless," he said laughing.

"Cut the crap and help me with these bags," Kevin said, apparently not liking the ribbing from Anthony.

"Seriously, how much does she know?" He asked.

"Just about everything," he replied, "I didn't tell her about our suspicions because they are just a long shot but there's one that we haven't eliminated."

"Good. Let's take it slow and hope that our "long shot" doesn't come to life." Anthony paused to look at his friend, then added, "I'm trying not to add to your beautiful day, but Mr. and Mrs. Johnston will be here shortly."

"You are really enjoying this."

"How many times do I get to see Mr. Wonderful squirm?"

"I didn't know you cared so much?"

"What are friends for?"

"Let's just get these bags in the house before princess cuts off the one I have left."

Once in the house Anthony pulled Danny into his arms and said, "I am so sorry Dan. This is a bad, bad situation, but you know that we will be right here for you." He kissed her forehead before releasing her to answer the door.

The doorbell rang to announce the arrival of the Johnstons. Whenever they entered into a room everyone present was aware of the air of power and dignity that surrounded them.

The 46-year-old ex-chief of police was 6'2 and carried his weight well. He was a very intimidating and watchful man. In contrast, his wife, Mrs. Johnston was short and stout. Although she was always fashionably dressed, she did not age as well as he did. However, no one ever saw her when she was not well dressed or with a bad hairdo. A hush came over the room as they entered. Everyone got the impression that Chief J, as he was often referred to, was not in the mood for any bull. After grunting some greetings and giving Kevin the stink eye he went right for his niece. Everyone left the room to give them some privacy, when Mrs. Johnston, who was lovingly called Miss Wilma, let out a deep soulful cry. The sound of her grief made everyone else cry too.

After a while, everyone returned to the living room except Lauren who went to the kitchen. She got busy making small sandwiches and iced tea for everyone. Miss Wilma came into the bright yellow kitchen to help or to take over.

Lauren smiled knowing the woman needed to do something, so she joined the rest of the crew in the living room.

Danny still looked beautiful even with red eyes and tear stained face. Lauren sat down beside her and held her hand. She felt so helpless not being able to help her friend, however, she understood that the only thing she could do was support her during this dreadful time.

As Lauren scanned the room, she could feel the tension in the air. Her brother was leaning against the mantel and staring out the window, Chief J, was looking at Kevin, and Teah was sniffling as she sat in one of the overstuffed chairs, Anthony was standing near his partner as if to silently say, "I've got your back."

A sigh of relief was felt by all as Miss Wilma entered the room carrying a tray of deli sandwiches she had made and glasses of iced tea. When she offered Danny a small plate of food, she said in a dry voice, "I'm not suicidal, Auntie, but I don't care if I ever eat again."

"Danielle Elizabeth Johnston!" Miss Wilma exclaimed with such strong disapproval in her voice that it startled everyone in the room.

Slamming the plate of food and drink that she was offering Danny on the oak coffee table in front of the couch, she sat next to her.

"You will not speak such language, and you will not think such thoughts! I've raised strong children! My children fight back when life is trying to bring them down! My children are strong in their faith! Are you still walking with God, Danny?! Don't hesitate, are you?!"

"Yes," Danny answered meekly as she felt the sting of her Auntie's words. She seldom spoke to her or Sam so seriously. Her scolding made Danny feel like a small child.

Danny's answer seemed to calm the older woman because her voice was lowered to a consoling tone. "Then you'll remember this verse from the Bible, "*weeping* may endure for a night, but *joy* cometh in the morning." Psalm 30:5. I know you know the bible, look it up, hang on to it. Understand this, I have lost one child, I don't intend to lose another…" her voice broke, and her husband pulled her into his arms where she wept as if her soul was breaking. Everyone in the room was sniffling, and the air was thick with grief and loss.

As usual, Miss Wilma's sad mood changed abruptly, she never wanted to appear to be weak or needy. She pulled away from her husband who was used to her sudden change from despair to "let's get down to business."

"Ok, we've got things to do."

She turned to Danny and said, "If it is alright with you, I would like for Jacob to make the funeral arrangements, and take care of all of that business."

"Yes, that is fine with me. I don't think I could get through it." Danny answered looking lovingly at the aunt and uncle who raised her. "But I need to go to Sam's to get the insurance papers and other things."

"No!" Kevin, Anthony, and her uncle all shouted at the same time.

Danny looked at them with a puzzled expression, "What? What is wrong?" Her puzzled expression turned to suspicion as she looked at their faces, all of which displayed impending doom.

"Ok, spill it!" Danny demanded.

Anthony walked to the end of the couch and in a no-nonsense voice, he explained, "Listen to me, Sis. The apartment is not cleared because of the ongoing investigation, and the police are still collecting evidence. Frankly, we don't know if it is a safe place for you to go right now. The person that committed this crime may return so, let us go over there to get what is needed."

She was looking at him intensely and weighing his every word. Satisfied that what he said made sense, she said, "I understand. Look Unc, I am ok with you handling everything, but I want to do something to help." However, looking at his face told her not to push the issue. She sighed and agreed.

"Ok. It is just as well because right now I am so tired, and all I want to do is sleep."

Everyone seemed to take a collective breath of relief. Feeling the break in the tension Lauren sprang into action. "Come on, let's get you a hot bath and some us time." She suggested. Then she looked at Teah. "Coming, Teah?"

"No, I just came over to tell Danny how sorry I am about Sam but right now I've got to pick up my mother from the hair salon. I'll be back, later." Teah said taking her keys as she wiped her eyes. "Hang in there Dan."

"Jay," Miss Wilma said to her husband, "I need to use the car to go to the Ladies' Auxiliary Committee meeting at the church to arrange the food for the funeral and days before."

"Wilma, I can pay for anything we need…"

"Then what will the auxiliary do? You don't want them to think that we are uppity or exclusive. Do you?" she asked sarcastically.

He smiled and replied, "Ok. I've got some stops then I'm going to Sam's." Realizing that he would not have a ride he looked at Kevin and Anthony and asked, "Guys, can I get a ride?"

Anthony spoke up, "Sure Chief." Then he said to Kevin, "We are not taking the cherished Lincoln." Kevin shook his head at his partner's jab at his car. "Let me kiss my sweet wife and then I will meet you outside."

Anthony drove a 1994 hunter green Pontiac Firebird that he equally cherished just as Kevin did his precious Lincoln. The only difference being that Anthony's car was more for showing off than Kevin's.

The house seemed less stressful with the excitement of the family and friends, Danny thought as she laid across the pillow top queen sized bed in the guestroom. She watched as Lauren moved between running water in the Jacuzzi bathtub and putting her clothes into the drawer chest and the dresser.

When she was finished putting Danny's things away she came to the bed and said, "We need to talk."

Danny knew from the sound of her voice and the look on her face that this talk would be about how she abandoned their friendship.

"You hurt me, Dan. You just left and didn't say goodbye." The level of her voice increased as she continued, "You didn't call me then worst of all, you didn't come to my wedding!"

Tears swelled in Danny's eyes. They ran down her face and begin to drop on the quilt.

"How could I? You got married two months after that night at the barbecue! I died that night, Lauren. I am still dead. I felt like he ripped my heart right out of my body and stomped on it!"

"That's him, Danny! What about me? Don't you think you owed me something? We have been friends since grade school. There wasn't a day that I wasn't with you. You were the sister I never had and I loved you."

"I didn't know what to do. I only knew that I could not be here."

"But my wedding, I always thought you would be my maid of honor."

Rising from the bed to look her friend in the eyes, "Really?! Oh, the idea sounds right for you and your

33

special day, but what would make that day so special for me?! Your brother, the man who crushed my world would walk you down the aisle and that is bad enough, but then I would have to look at your knocked-up sister-in-law. How is that good for me?! How would being in touch with you help me heal, Lauren?" Her voice got louder as she talked about her feelings for the first time in four years. "What would we have to talk about? Baby showers, baby shopping…?"

"Stop!" Lauren shouted, going over to her visibly shaken friend, pulling her to sit on the edge of the bed. "Calm down, Danny. So, in 4 years you have not dealt with this situation?"

"I won't let myself think about what happened between Kevin and me. I couldn't come to your wedding. I couldn't come home. I wouldn't be here now if Sam…" She realizes that she couldn't say the words killed, murdered, died or dead when she talked about Sam. "Unc and Auntie always came to visit me. They never talked about it either." She sniffled.

"Danny, you have got to deal with this." Looking into her pain filled eyes, Lauren stressed, "You have to deal with Kevin."

Turning away from her friend, sighed and she said, "I don't know how."

"Look at me Danny, do you still love him?"

Danny turned to look at her friend and replied, "I don't think I can ever stop loving him, nor, can I stop hurting from what he did to me – to us. This on top of Sam's death is too much for me. I know Auntie told me that *weeping may endure for a night, but joy cometh in the morning,* but my night of weeping never stops."

"Then hold on to this Bible verse it helped me through the painful time when I was recovering from the accident. I couldn't understand why it happened to me. I am a good person. I felt that I've never purposely hurt anyone, so why was this happening to me but then I remembered this Bible verse, Proverbs 3:5-6, *Trust in the LORD with all your heart, And lean not on your own understanding; In all your ways acknowledge Him, And He shall direct your paths.* This verse has comforted me through all of my hard times. Even when things happened that made me think, why did God let that happen? I just remember that verse and go on with my life. I may not ever understand why somethings happened, but I know there's a God so, I lean not on my own understanding. Don't you remember when we had to learn this verse in St. James Baptist Church's summer Bible school?"

Wiping her face with the tissue Lauren handed her she laughed, "Yes, but we went every year to look at the cute boys and for the cool Sunday school picnic trips."

Lauren laughed, too. "But we did learn more about The Lord and church discipline. Those were good days." Standing up she took Danny's hands and said," Come on, let's get you soaking in this delightful bathtub while I run to the store. Then she turned to Danny, "After all of this is over with Sam, Danny, you must face this situation with Kevin and fix it. Somehow you must find the strength to confront him because I will not lose my sister again. Promise me."

"I will. I promise."

"Now, I have to go to the pharmacy to get my migraine medicine refilled. I will be right back."

"You still have those headaches? I thought they would be gone by now. Are you having one now?"

"No. Well, I feel one coming on, and I have to take the medication to keep it from coming all the way. I'm okay."

"Am I causing it?" Danny asked suddenly feeling guilty for causing her friend to be in pain.

"Of course not," Lauren reassured her. She quickly redirected Danny's attention as she'd done many times before. This time, it was to keep down her self-inflicted guilt of imposing on other people. "Now, bath time, Missy. I will be right back."

CHAPTER THREE

Soaking in the big tub, feeling the jets spraying water on her body, Danny started to relax. She felt guilty about Lauren's headaches because she knew that extreme stress could trigger them. Smiling, Danny knew the migraines would never make Lauren feel like a victim. She would fight anyone that tried to make her condition a limited situation in her life except Anthony. He didn't seem to breathe until he knew for sure that Lauren would survive the injuries she'd suffered from the accident.

Leaning back in the tub, Danny started remembering the day of the car wreck. It always amazed her how people could recall where they were and what they were doing when something tragic happened. It was just getting dark on August 29, 1990, she and Teah had just left the library where Teah had just passed the reading part of the High school Diploma Assessment. Teah was over the moon with the results of the test. Kevin had let her drive his 1990 Lincoln for the first time that day so, she and Teah were riding in style. Thinking back she thought of how he had always driven a Lincoln. Maybe he thought that car enhanced his *mysterious* personality.

As soon as they entered into the car Danny's cellphone began to ring. It was Kevin instructing her to meet him at Jewish Hospital. His voice was so controlled and rigid that she knew that something was very wrong.

Turning on more hot water Danny continued to recall that awful day. Her heart still clenched remembering how she had begged rather than asked Kevin if he was okay. When he confirmed that he was alright, a new sense of dread had filled her belly. She didn't recognize her own voice as she asked or demanded, "What is it, Kevin?" But his voice remained distant and restrained while he gave her specific instructions, "Danny, meet me in the back parking lot of Jewish Hospital. Drive carefully and concentrate on the road." Then he promptly broke the connection.

She could remember how long she sat there until she became aware of Teah shouting "What? What is wrong!?" She could see that Teah was becoming hysterical as Danny tried to mimic Kevin to put her at ease. However, she did drive the Lincoln through town faster than Kevin would have approved but something was very wrong, and she had the feeling that the news would tear her apart.

When they arrived in the hospital's parking lot, Kevin met them and told them that Lauren had been in a car accident with a drunk driver. He further explained that she may not make it through the night. Danny flinched in the tub still hearing herself screaming and sinking to the ground. After a while, she became aware that Kevin and Teah were on the floor of the parking lot with her trying to calm her down. Coming to herself she looked at Kevin, who was crying too because Lauren is his sister! Teah was trying to console both of them. Sometimes people think individuals with disabilities do not have the capabilities to function in any situation, but both Kevin and Danny learned something about Teah, that day. She called them both to the task.

"Look, you both are acting like Lauren is already dead. She needs your strength now, and so does Anthony and your mother! If you go into the hospital like this then you are not giving hope to Lauren or to them, so pull it together!"

They looked at her with amazement and walked into the hospital with renewed attitudes. All of them stayed in the ICU waiting room praying that Lauren would pull through while Captain Johnston terrorized the drunk driver.

By the grace and mercy of God, Lauren made it through the night and continued to make progress. Lauren was always tiny, but she had lost more weight which concerned all of them.

Lindsey showed up two days later with fresh, fashionable gowns, slippers and personal hygiene products for Lauren. She just pranced right into Lauren's room and transformed her from the living dead to the thriving living.

Lauren was released from the hospital with strict physical therapy instructions. Lindsey appointed herself as Lauren's physical therapy coach. She was so relentless with the exercise and goals that Danny nearly stepped in to put a stop to what seemed like punishment and torture but Lauren continued to rise to meet the challenge.

Danny was in charge of Lauren's cool down routines, massages, and baths. Mrs. Williams filtered phone calls, prepared medications and managed the Women's Auxiliary.

All in all, Lauren had recovered, although she still suffered from debilitating migraine headaches. She understood that the headaches were something she would have to live with, but she refused to be victimized by them. Lauren took control of her life and was determined not to let the migraines stop her from doing anything that she wanted to do. The threat of Migraines would not control her life.

The water seemed to wash all of her stress away. She began to feel stronger. Taking the stroll down memory lane caused her to think about taking control of her life. While she washed her body with a large bath lily and nice smelling soap that Lauren had insisted she use, she thought that it was time for her to start making some decisions for herself and start being more responsible for her life. Danny decided that only the strong survived, and she was going to be strong. She'd go to Sam's apartment to get her insurance papers and other important papers from her safe, then maybe everyone would see how sturdy she really was.

Dressed in a pink and black Nike warm-up suit, with matching tennis shoes, Danny left Lauren's house. Sam's apartment was on the other side of Shawnee Park so, she decided to jog through the park because it was still daylight, and she needed the exercise. She justified it all as she set a steady pace. She wasn't afraid of the danger of being alone in the park for she had taken measures to ensure her safety. Before leaving her best friend's house, she had searched for a small gun to carry with her. Anthony, a gun lover, had them all over the house. It didn't take long for Danny to find the right size gun. It was a North American Guardian 32 automatic, it had a wood handle and to her delight, it had a ready holster. Her uncle had taught her and Sam all about guns such as, how to use them and how to be safe with them.

She had to hook the gun holster to the back of her pink sports bra because it was too heavy for the pockets of her jogging suit, then she made sure the hood of the suit covered the bump the gun made under the jacket. This was not the first time she had secured a weapon in this manner; she did it all the time when she ran in Berkeley, California. Aunt Wilma and Unc had made sure she continued her education after the tragic breakup between her and Kevin, and the University of California fit perfectly with her situation.

While jogging through the park, Danny noticed how simple life seemed for everyone. Elderly couples sitting on the porch talking to their neighbors, men tending to their yards while children played ball. Every once in a while she could hear mothers calling for their children to come in and eat dinner. Yes, it seemed as if life was going on as usual while her world was crumbling, but she was taking steps to change all of that today.

Rounding the bend in the road, she could see Sam's apartment building, and her heart leaped with anticipation.

The person was in Sam's apartment reliving the murder. Sitting in the body outline drawn on the floor by police with white tape, the person was stabbing the area where Sam's body had fallen.

"Die bitch! Die! Die!" the person whispered loudly. Stabbing the place where Sam had died over and over.

Pretending to be Sam the person continued, "No! Please don't hurt me! Please! Please!"

"No, bitch you must die! You must die! Die..." The person heard the key turning in the front door, so they ran to hide in the pantry.

Danny walked into Sam's ground floor apartment, halfway expecting a squeal and a great big hug from her. The realization struck her that that would no longer be possible. Her heart seized causing her to whimper out loud.

Tears still gathered in her eyes as she looked around the small, bright, and airy living room. Sam didn't like clutter, just a lot of open space. The furnishings were simple and strategically placed in order to give the room a wide look of freedom. Everything in the room was there to induce a calm sense of peace but Sam would soon be resting in eternal peace. That thought seemed to stab her in the stomach.

"No," she said to herself trying to regain her emotions.

"Let's just get what I came for and get out of here but maybe everyone was right about me not coming to the apartment."

Leaving the cozy living room, she went to Sam's bedroom. Pictures of her favorite singers in various forms of dress or undress hung on the beige walls. Danny sat on the bed taking the room in for the last time because she knew she would never come back here again.

On one side table was an 8 x 10 picture of their parents. Danny picked it up to study it carefully. Their Mom had on a summer dress, she was looking at their dad lovingly, and their dad looked so handsome in his U. S. Army uniform. Sighing, she put the picture back on the table. On the other side table was an 8 x 10 picture of Sam and Slicks. Honestly, Slicks? This is what they all called Sam's bad-boy friend with benefits. On the dresser were various pictures of Danny and Sam. Looking at the pictures, Danny's heart ached from the loss of her sister. Almost becoming emotional again, she pushed the sadness aside and focused on the purpose of this visit. Walking to the large painting of the sun setting between clouds, Danny pulled the picture from the wall where the safe was hidden.

She opened the safe and began looking for Sam's birth certificate, Social Security card, and insurance papers when she heard a sound behind her. Turning around Danny saw the most hideous being running toward her with a long shiny knife. Quickly, she dropped the papers and rolled across the bed to the other side. The monstrous thing started across the bed, but backed away when it saw that Danny had drawn the gun.

The person in this repulsive costume stood there looking at Danny. Through a full head mask that looked like a character from the *Night of the Living Dead*, it spoke through a wide mouth with long sharp teeth, "I was going to take my time with you, but since you are here, I'll have to make this quick." It must have had something in its mouth to make the voice sound terrifying, but Danny remained focused on not letting this disgusting creature take her life.

Then it started across the bed again. This time, Danny fired the gun into the bed as a warning and the strangely dressed person leapt off of the bed.

Danny's heart was beating wildly in her chest, for she was sure that this creature had killed her sister. The person's face was concealed by the Zombie mask, and it was wearing a purple scarf around the neck and green army fatigues. The hand that held the tactical combat knife was covered with a black glove which exposed the fingers.

Danny knew that she had to focus because this ghoulish thing intended to kill her. The shot had made it retreat to regroup, but its goal clearly was to kill her.

"That gun can't stop me. You will die today." The demon faced freak with the creepy voice started across the bed again. This time, Danny fired three bullets into the chest of this unexplainable being. The person fell face down on the bed, Danny ran out of the bedroom and down the hall to the kitchen. She hid in the pantry but didn't close the door, because it might make a noise that would give away her position. She knew that she had hit the disgusting creature in the chest with three bullets, but she wasn't taking any chances. Like in most horror stories the monster may seem to be dead but then comes back to life and proceeds to kill the victim. Not today, she thought. I will wait to see what happens. She kept the gun trained on the entry way of the kitchen from the living room.

The person should be dead or hurt, Danny thought as she knelt on the floor and listened intensely for noises of any type. But suddenly, she heard the sound of footsteps coming from the back kitchen door, and at the same time the Zombie face with its fluorescent yellow hair, large black eyes, and even larger mouth appeared in the kitchen window saying, "This ain't over, bitch!"

Coming out of the pantry, Danny fired two more shots at the person through the kitchen window. Then, someone dressed all in black tackled her, knocking her to the ground and the gun slid under the table, far from her reach.

Even though the former Chief was retired, everyone respected him like he still had an active command and that basically meant striving hard not to get on his bad side. Tonight and the rest of the week Kevin would have to stay out of his path but how would he do that when there was a war brewing between Kevin and the Chief's niece? Not to mention the fact that one of his nieces had been murdered. Kevin was not in a comfortable place and being enclosed with the Chief in a small car was not helping foster a respectful relationship.

"So, thoughts on Sam's murder?" Chief J asked.

"It's early in the investigation, but we have some suspects in mind," Anthony answered. "Sir, was Sam dating anyone special?"

"She was dating, but nothing serious. There was always Slicks," He said with distaste in his voice.

That is probably how he speaks of me, Kevin thought as Anthony pulled in front of the Chief's house.

"I'll only be a minute. " Chief J said getting out of the small car and walking toward his house.

When the door closed, Anthony turned to Kevin, who was in the back seat and said, "What do you think about Slicks? Could he have killed Sam?"

"Are you kidding?" Kevin answered, "He loved that girl, and she loved him. He just wouldn't leave the streets for her."

"But think of this," Anthony continued, "What if he thought she was serious about another man?"

"Nah, he knew she was dating other men. Last I heard, she was dating a doctor from the hospital where she worked." Kevin replied.

"Let's bring both of them in and have a sit-down."

"What about the Chief? How much should we let him know about the case?" Anthony asked with concern.

He was interrupted by a dispatch call.

"This is Porter," Anthony answered.

"There are reports of shots fired at 4530 West Broadway. This address is the scene of an ongoing investigation." the dispatcher informed.

Anthony motioned for Kevin, who was listening carefully, to get Chief J. Anthony continued to get information from the dispatcher, while Kevin ran into the Chief's house.

Chief J was strapping on a gun holster when Kevin ran into the room. "We've got to go! Shots were fired at Sam's apartment!"

Asking no questions, Jacob Johnston picked up his 40 cal Smith and Wesson, holstered it, and ran with Kevin to the car. Only this time, he got into the back of the car, he knew that this was official LPD business.

As the green muscle car sped away from the curve, Anthony told Kevin to request that a police car be sent to his house. Turning on the lights and siren, Anthony headed at high speed to Samantha's apartment.

Danny could hear the sirens and she knew that they were headed her way, but they were much too far away for her to be hopeful, so she fought harder with the stranger for her life. At this point in the scuffle, Danny had punched the intruder in the throat so hard that he went down gasping for air. Unlike her first encounter, she knew that this was a man because he had an extremely hard body, and he just smelled like a man. She raised her foot to assault his manhood when he surprised her by grabbing it and twisting it so that she would fall down.

As she jumped up from the floor, she heard footsteps running toward her once again and this only confused her further. This time they were coming to the kitchen where she was engaged in a battle with a strange man. The man was still trying to get his breath when Danny kicked him in the head and attacked the new person who had come through the door. Her fist connected with the new intruder, but she ended up in a headlock. Breathing hard, she stomped on the person's foot. He yelled but did not let her go. As she tried again, someone turned on the kitchen lights. Police swarmed into the small kitchen pointing guns and shouting commands at the man who was now on the floor trying to breathe.

Realizing that he had the woman he loved in a headlock, he released her, but he kept her arms pinned to her sides. "Danny! Stop fighting! It's over! Calm down!" Kevin shouted.

Relief washed over her at hearing Kevin's voice, but that relief was cut short when she looked down at the floor and saw the chalk outline where her sister had fallen and died.

She screamed in a pitch that will never be forgotten by anyone who was in the tiny kitchen. The police officers were handcuffing the man who had now been identified as Ace, Slicks younger brother but they stopped to see why she was screaming. Tears came to the former Chief's eyes as he barked, "Take her out of her here, Kevin. An ambulance is on the way."

There was no reasoning with Danny. Seeing all the blood in the chalk body outline was her undoing. She was fighting Kevin, trying to get to the place where her sister died.

Kevin ended up carrying her from the apartment like one would carry a baby. She had stopped fighting, but she was still crying hysterically.

Kevin noticed that a crowd had gathered outside of the apartment building as he carried Danny to the ambulance. Another ambulance drove up and parked behind the first one. The second one had been sent to treat Ace. Officers were trying to keep the crowds back while paramedics tried to stabilize Danny. She wouldn't let go of Kevin, so he got in the ambulance with her and closed the door. Once in the ambulance, the screaming and mournful crying continued. The paramedics tried in vain to communicate with her but got nowhere in their attempts. Kevin held her while they injected her with a sedative. Thanks to the next of kin being on site the paramedic didn't have to wait to treat her. Being extremely upset was causing her blood pressure to spike often and was putting her health in danger.

The second ambulance pulled off transporting Ace to the nearest hospital. Anthony and the other officers left the scene to meet the ambulance at the hospital.

After a half an hour of trying in vain to calm Danny, the medics wanted to transport her, but Kevin asked them to wait until he talked to her uncle.

Chief J. was standing outside the ambulance with his hands in his pockets. Walking towards him, Kevin thought that the man looked calm and as always, in control, but as he got closer, he could see that his eyes were troubled.

"She's calming down some, but her blood pressure is all over the place. The medics want to transport her." Kevin explained. "But I don't think that's a good idea. We can protect her better in a private setting than in a public setting. I'm taking her to Lauren's. She's a Nurse Practitioner and Danny's best friend. I think that is what she needs now."

"Will she be safe there?" The Chief asked, noting that Kevin hadn't asked him if he could take her to Lauren's house.

"As safe as if she was in Fort Knox," Kevin replied. "I will be there. Anthony has sent cars to the house. Lauren and I are experts with firearms. It's the safest place I know."

"I will be there as soon as I can. I've got to see what the hell was going on here. I need to talk to Ace. Don't let her out of your sight." Looking at the various news station vans pulling up to the crime scene, he barked, "The media is here; get her out of here, now."

Right at that moment, to Kevin's relief, Lauren pulled up beside the ambulance in Kevin's Lincoln. Moments later, Kevin slid Danny's trembling body across the front seat of the big car. Lauren was in the back of the car leaning forward into the front seat to comfort Danny. Neither of them had ever seen Danny this helpless, and it was cause for great concern. Lauren pulled the EMS blanket over her best friend's shoulders and rubbed her arms as Kevin drove the shiny Lincoln quickly and carefully around the curves of Southwestern Parkway to his sister's house.

Her head was rested on Kevin's right thigh. Her eyes looked straight ahead, and the tears were still streaming down her face. She was holding his hand like it was a lifeline to her being.

Kevin pulled the Lincoln across the lawn, nearly to the front door of the house. Lauren was out of the car as soon as it stopped. Together they helped Danny into the house and into the guest bedroom. Kevin took her shoes off and put her under the covers while Lauren went to get her medical bag. The room was eerily quiet except for the small whimpering sounds that Danny was making.

Kevin's heart was breaking. He wanted to make all of this just go away, but knowing he couldn't just frustrated him more. His heart beat wildly knowing that someone wanted to kill Danny, too. "What the hell is going on?!" His mind screamed.

Lauren returned with the medical bag and proceeded to take Danny's blood pressure.

"It's going down some," Lauren said with relief. "Keep rubbing her and talking to her. I am going to take some migraine medicine. Don't tell Anthony."

"Do you need to lie down? I …"

"No, I am fine. Just keep her calm." Lauren said as she hurried off to get the medication that would stop the pain beginning in front of her head.

CHAPTER FOUR

Lauren was on her way to the bedroom to get the migraine medicine she had just bought but she didn't get a chance to take it because the doorbell rang. When she opened the door, she was met with an out of breath and visibly upset Miss Wilma carrying pans of food.

"What happened?" She asked breathlessly, "Is she alright?! Where is she?"

Taking the pan of food from her, Lauren explained, "She was attacked at Sam's apartment."

"What? What was she doing at Sam's place?"

"Miss Wilma, she is here in the guest room with Kevin. She is very upset and it is affecting her blood pressure. See what you can do and I'll be in later to check it."

Miss Wilma rushed to the guestroom. When Danny saw Aunt Wilma, she started to cry again.

Laying on the bed with Danny and Kevin she said soothingly, "You're safe now, Danny. Come on, free your mind. We will not let anything happen to you. Let me wash your face and get you out of those clothes."

Kevin took the clue and left the room while Miss Wilma fussed over Danny. On his way to check on his sister the doorbell rang again. This time it was Teah.

"I just heard! It's all over the news! Where is she, Kevin? Is she alright?"

"Calm down, Teah. She is fine. Miss Wilma is with her now."

Sitting down on one of the overstuffed chairs, Teah asked, "What happened?"

Taking a seat on the sofa across from her, Kevin looked at her for a moment, thinking about how much he should tell her. Danny was attacked by known or unknown persons. Teah could be a suspect. Teah had started to let her real feelings about Danny and himself be known. Here lately she had begun to let it be known that she would like it very much if he remained married to Lindsey, but just how far would she go to make that happen?

"Kevin, what happened?" Teah asked again.

"Danny was attacked at Sam's apartment." He replied watching her face.

"Oh my God! Is she alright?"

She looked genuinely shocked, Kevin thought, but that could be an act. He always considered her to be the group's drama queen.

A puzzled look came over her face, she asked, "Kevin are you alright? Oh, you are probably upset about Danny. I know you have some feelings for her, but you are married to Lindsey. Must I remind you of that?" She scolded, standing up. "I know that Danny has problems, but you have a wife now…"

Kevin stood up, "I am not having this conversation with you. Get out!"

The guestroom door opened and Miss Wilma came into the living room, "What the hell is going on out here? Let's tone it down. I've finally got Danny to sleep."

Teah spoke up in the self-righteous voice she is known for and said, "Miss Wilma, you will back me. Kevin needs to leave Danny alone and go home to his wife. She has been waiting for him to call her all day. You know this ain't right."

"What the hell are you talking about!?" The older lady shouted, "The only person I care about right now is Danny. If he is what will make her better, then she shall have him. By the way, what business is this of yours? Why are you hating on your friend?"

"Oh, so now that she is home, all of your Bible talk just stops! What happened to "Marriage is honorable in all, and the bed undefiled: but whoremongers and adulterers God will judge, Hebrews 13:4. Or thy shalt not covet thy neighbor's wife or thy shalt not commit adultery, Exodus 20:13!" She shouted.

Lauren heard all of the shouting and ran into the room.

"What is the problem in here?" she asked.

"Your friend has lost her mind. Instead of being concerned about the attack on Danny, she is carrying on about Danny and Kevin." Miss Wilma answered.

"I told you earlier today that you won't do this in my house!" Lauren hissed.

Seeing that there was no reasoning with Teah, Miss Wilma opened the front door and asked the officers outside to step into the house.

Teah continued to shout out Bible quotes to make her point about Kevin and Danny.

Kevin stood alert and watched the conflict escalate, but he chose not to intervene because he wanted to observe this person of interest. Teah was far too involved in his love life, and she seemed to be showing a great dislike for Danny.

Miss Wilma said to officers, "Escort her off of this property. She is out of control."

"What? Me? I am just pointing out to all ya'll, that he is married!" she screamed. "He can't treat Lindsey like that!"

"Leave or I will have you arrested," Lauren said firmly.

"Arrested? You bitch! You never liked Lindsey or me anyway, it was always Danny!"

"Officers. Please!" Miss Wilma commanded.

"Let's go, ma'am. We don't want a scene." The Officer warned.

Anthony and Chief J had pulled into the driveway just in time to see the Officers escorting Teah to her car that was parked on the street.

Closing the door, Wilma Johnston realized that she must take over this situation to restore some sort of order and calmness. Lauren looked as if her head would explode, and she knew she had to head off Anthony (no pun intended). He was very protective of his wife, who was very protective of her best friend.

"Lauren, I want you to go into the guest room with Danny, turn off the lights and go to sleep so that headache will go away. Did you take the medication?"

Everyone knew about Lauren's headaches. The medicine helped, but only if she took it at the onset of the migraine. Miss Wilma knew that Anthony helped her to control this condition. Sometimes the headaches were so severe that he had to take her to the emergency room. Therefore, he always made sure he was on top of this because he could not stand to see her suffer.

"I just took it but I can't lay down now, I've got to get ready for visitors…"

Putting her hand up, Miss Wilma interrupted, "I am putting in a call to the Ladies Auxiliary. They will be glad to take over. Don't worry about anything. Now scoot before that bear-of-a-husband gets a look at you."

Gratefully, Lauren left the living room for the guestroom. She really needed to get a handle on this headache before Anthony shut her down or Danny needed her.

"Kevin, you are going to take this police talk to the Que Shack. People will be coming, and I don't want them to hear about this investigation firsthand."

"Good idea, but I want an officer in the house because I can't take any more chances."

"Plain clothes, please. We have to keep up appearances. Now, check on Danny, make sure Lauren is laying down and then get the posse to the Que Shack."

Although Miss Wilma was a short woman about 5'2, she had a strong presence. When she spoke, people moved. She had a no-nonsense tone, and no one wanted to argue with her when she was in her command mode.

When Kevin opened the door of the dark room, he could see Danny was on her stomach sleeping hard and his sister lying on her side with a protective hand on Danny. As he left to intercept his crew, he noticed a plainclothes officer entering the house. Miss Wilma works fast, he thought. With a policeman in the house and the officers outside he was satisfied that Danny was safe for the moment.

CHAPTER FIVE

"Miss Wilma is in charge of the house and the girls, and we've been banished to the Que Shack," Kevin said walking to the driveway.

"That's good," Anthony agreed, "We need to talk."

"I need a drink," Chief J stated.

The Que Shack was a small dwelling in the back of the Porter home. Anthony was known for his famous Derby and Fourth of July cookouts, so all of the equipment needed to make the big bash happen year after year was stored in the Que Shack. But as the years passed, the Shack had evolved into a man-cave. All of the men were impressed with the work Anthony had put into the shack. It did not look like a shack at all. It was like a mini house. The porch of the dull blue structure was painted white, and Anthony had put a new roof on the building. His hobby most days was seeing how much comfort he could put into his man-cave.

As they stepped inside, they saw more improvement. Instead of a cooler for beverages, there was a shiny new refrigerator. A flat screen television and a white board lined one of the walls, and a small bar dominated another wall. Sprinkled throughout the little shack were various pictures of him and Lauren. He put a lot of comforts into his home away from home. Kevin wondered how much time he did spend out here.

"Are you planning to live here?" Kevin asked.

Anthony laughed as he handed a glass and a bourbon bottle to Chief J, "No. Just want my pals to enjoy my famous cookouts in style.

Kevin went to the refrigerator and got a cold beer. After pouring himself a hefty sized shot of bourbon, Chief J sat on a nearby bar stool and asked, "What the hell is going on?"

"Hell, if I know," Kevin answered shaking his head. Drinking the shot straight down the former Chief aired his frustrations. "Do you know how close I came to losing her?" He shouted trying to keep himself in check.

Anthony and Kevin were shocked; they never thought Chief J had any feelings.

"It's okay, sir," Kevin said. "I know how you feel. I thought I couldn't live if something happened to Dan."

"What did happen? We couldn't talk to Ace because Ace literally can't talk. Danny nearly killed him. Is he the one?" Anthony asked taking a swig from his beer can.

All heads turned at the sound of someone knocking on the door of the shack. Slicks put his head in and asked, "Can I come in?" Chief J took two giant steps and roughly grabbed Slicks by his collar and jerked him inside the shack, "Yes, get the hell in here and tell us why your brother attacked my niece."

Anthony and Kevin pulled the big man away from Slicks. "Wait, let's see what he has to say." Anthony suggested.

Rubbing his chest where the man he feared had grabbed him Slicks complained, "Look, I came here to explain, man! I didn't come for no bullshit. What the Hell Mr. J?"

"So, explain," Kevin said, keeping an eye on Chief J, who was ready to explode.

"Ace didn't attack Danny. He was trying to save her."

"Save her?" They all said.

"Yeah man, I don't know what happened to Sam, so I was trying to find out. I had some of my boys watching the crib, you know how people break in a crime scene to steal stuff or I thought that sick bastard that killed Sam might come back. I also had some of my people watching Danny. When I got the call that she was on the move, I knew she was on her way to Sam's crib." He stopped talking and looked at the Chief. "I didn't ..." there was a catch in his voice. He seemed to be trying to collect his emotions. "I would never hurt Sam or Danny. I love Sam." Tears were swelling in his eyes.

After a moment, Anthony said, "Sit down. Take a moment." Then he gave Chief J a warning look.

"Beer or bourbon?" Kevin asked.

"Beer." Slicks answered never taking his eyes off of the big man who had just tried to hang him with his big hands.

He accepted an open beer from Kevin and nearly downed it.

Continuing Slicks said, "Then I got a call saying that someone was inside the apartment. Man, I was driving as fast as I could, but I didn't get there in time to help. By the time I got there, I was told to go to the hospital because Ace was hurt. Now I ask you, what the hell is going on?"

Ignoring his question, Chief Johnston asked, "Why did you have Danny tailed?"

"Sam is … was a Nurse's Assistant at the hospital for the drug rehab service. She saw many weirdos and whacked-out people. I kept telling her to quit, but no, she was trying to save the world as usual. Then out of the blue, she called me the other day."

"What did she want?" Anthony asked.

"She was upset because one of the doctors talked crazy to her." His lips turned into a cruel smile he added, "He won't talk crazy to her again, and I don't know if it was him or not.

Speaking of crazy, get this, Ace said the dude that attacked Danny was dressed in a Halloween costume."

"What?!" Chief Johnston asked.

"I know, it's strange, ask Wes. He chased it when it ran from the apartment. Ask Danny."

"Still, how did you know that Danny might be a target?" Kevin asked.

"I really didn't, but I couldn't take any chances. I don't know who killed Sam, but I knew Danny would either try to find out who did or she would do something that would put herself in danger so, I asked my boys to watch out for her."

"How soon can we talk to your brother? " Kevin asked.

"Soon I guess. He talked to me by writing on paper. The doc says it's not as bad as they first thought. He will be laid up for a few days, but he will be okay when the swelling goes down. Danny nearly whopped his ass. " Slicks said with amusement.

There was another knock on the door, this time, it was their boss, the current Chief of Police, Brandon Taylor and a great friend to the former chief.

After the greeting, the current Chief said, "Okay, so what happened?" Looking at Slicks, he asked, "Is this a suspect?"

Anthony said, "This is Slicks. Samantha dated him off and on. His real name is Sylvester Malone."

Chief Taylor stood back to take a good look at Slicks, then he asked, again, "Is he a suspect?"

"Not at this moment, sir. He was just explaining what he knows about the attack." Anthony answered.

Offended by Anthony's answer, Slicks questioned, "What do you mean at this moment? Me and my boys were the ones trying to save your girl."

Chief Taylor asked, "How did you know she needed saving?"

Slicks felt that he was being disrespected, and he really didn't like the po-po or the way he was being treated so, he decided to piss them off.

"Because these bros don't know their women." He boasted.

"What?" Kevin and Anthony said at once.

Chief J just observed Slicks' change in behavior. He never understood what Samantha saw in this jerk. He was "straight-up hood". But what was his real deal? He was 5'7 which is an average size so, it couldn't be short man syndrome. The big baggy, dark clothing made him look intimidating. Obviously, this was the look he was going for and now the attitude. The one thing Chief J knew for sure was that Slicks didn't kill Sam. He loved her, but he couldn't change his ways to have a normal relationship with her. What did she see in this hood rat? Maybe he didn't want to know, he concluded.

"Look, man, a blind man could have told you that Danny was going to do something. Girlfriend was not going to sit still while you dote all over her. She ain't that kind. I didn't know she would be attacked, but I knew she would do something." Just to rub it in Kevin's face he asked, "Why didn't you, Mister big time Lieutenant of homicide?"

Moving at the speed of light Kevin left the bar stool that he was sitting on and grabbed Slicks by the neck.

This time, Anthony and Chief Taylor saved Slicks from bodily harm by pulling Kevin back.

But Slicks wasn't through, rubbing his neck he said, "At the risk of being a victim of police brutality, I will continue. I just got here and took one look at your wife, and I knew her head was about to blow off her shoulders." Chief J put his arm out to keep Anthony in his seat.

"Since I'm on a roll I might as well piss off everyone. Chief Johnston, why didn't you know about the Doc that threatened Sam? Why did she have to come to me? You being top Mister X Popo? Maybe she didn't think you could handle it, with your advanced age and all."

Chief Johnston got up from his chair and started walking toward Slicks. No one tried to intervene this time, secretly each of them hoped that the 6'4 man punched his lights out. At least it wouldn't officially be police brutality.

"That's enough, Slicks!" Chief Johnston hissed in his most dangerous voice. "I *let* you have your say so, I can tell you this; I think you are a suspect because Sam wouldn't be with you anymore. She wanted an educated man like the doctor, someone in her field, someone she could be proud of, not a hoodlum like you. You couldn't take it that she didn't want you anymore."

Chief Johnston stood very close to him and continued, "If I find that this is true, life as you know it, as pitiful as your life is, will be over for you."

Slicks was frozen in place. He was aware that he had gone too far, but he didn't like people looking down their noses at him. Nobody knew his story and anyway, who were they to judge him? Sam never judged him. She saw the good in him. Tears came to his eyes, but he stopped them from falling. Not here, Slicks thought, he would never let this group of men see him cry.

As Chief J stood in front of Slicks, he saw the cockiness turn to fear and the fear turn to sadness, but now the cockiness was back.

Slicks decided to cut his losses and step back from the tall, intimidating man. Holding his palms up and open, he slowly lifted his arms away from his side, Slicks said, "Calm down, Chief J. I'm about to go to the house now. Miss Wilma is fixing me a plate, and I intend to get down with some good eating. Y'all take it easy now." As he backed out the door, he added, "Like I said earlier, keep an eye on your women."

"You're still a suspect so, be where I can find you," Anthony warned Slicks as he left the shack. Slicks never replied.

CHAPTER SIX

Lauren woke with a start, not used to sleeping in the guest room, she was a little disorientated. Then she remembered the tragic events of the day. She had nearly lost her best friend. Realization set in so she reached out and touched Danny's shoulder just to be sure that she was still in the bed and that she was still asleep.

Knowing that someone was trying to kill her best friend was stomach cramping scary. Lauren also knew that Anthony and Kevin would not stop until the person who killed Sam and tried to kill Danny was brought to justice.

Right now it felt good to have her friend at home and safe for the moment. However, she and Danny would have to have a heart to heart talk about her decision to go to Sam's apartment alone. What was she thinking?

Turning on the large lamp on the night stand, Lauren checked Danny's pulse as she continued to sleep soundly. Lauren smiled as she let her limp arm fall back to the bed. After checking her blood pressure, Lauren turned off the light and left the room.

Going into the kitchen Lauren was startled to see that Miss Wilma had cleaned the kitchen and was putting the food away.

"Oh. Miss Wilma," Lauren cried, "I feel so guilty…"

But Miss Wilma interrupted, "No, you don't. This is what families do for each other. Now go wash your face and I'll warm you some food."

"But…" Lauren tried to say.

"Go on, now." The older woman insisted, "You've got to feed that strong medication you take."

Giving up, Lauren went to the bathroom and washed her face. The pain of the headache was gone, but she felt the groggy after effects. At least Anthony wouldn't give her a hard time about not taking the medication, she thought.

Drying off her face Lauren thought about Miss Wilma. The forty-five-year-old woman had not aged as well as her husband, but he loved her as if she looked like Janet Jackson. Chief J was a very sexy man, Lauren thought drying her hands. Very much a man's man but he loved his wife. She often marveled at how Miss Wilma was such a strong woman. A pleasant person, but when she spoke, people listened. The woman could take any chaotic situation and turn it into a smooth operation. Thanks to Miss Wilma, the day had gone well, and she seemed to do this without any effort.

Lauren was still feeling the after effects of the powerful migraine medication she had taken earlier as she returned to the kitchen. There on the island was her plate of soul food made by the best of the best, the Ladies Auxiliary Committee of Ephesians Baptist Church. This group of ladies prided themselves on preparing meals for any opportunity. Each member had a specialty dish created with a pass down of secret ingredients that no one could duplicate. Setting before her was a heart attack on a plate. The macaroni and cheese made by the deacon's wife, Sister Delores Harris, chicken and dumplings made by Sister Anne-Marie Brown. Lauren could see the ladies smiling as they presented their outstanding dishes. The baked chicken and cornbread dressing made with loving hands by Sister Dianne Thomas and candied sweet potatoes prepared by the pastor's wife, Elise Smith. Fatback and collard greens made by Sister Wilma Johnston, the president of the senior choir, and to top that off, homemade sweet potato pie, made by Clara Mayfield the church's secretary.

Being in the health industry, Lauren always ate healthy, but today she needed comfort food, so she dove in to the food, swimming with great-guilt-calories, to smooth her nerves, tummy and the lingering side effects of the medication.

Miss Wilma sat on the side of the kitchen island sipping coffee.

"You are looking better. How do you feel?" Miss Wilma asked.

"I have medicine-head, but I must say I feel much better after some sleep. I can't thank you enough for taking over this afternoon." Looking out of her large kitchen window, she could see that it was early evening. The lights were on in the Que shack, which meant an important meeting of the minds was at play. "Well, all day. I must have slept longer than I thought."

"No. You needed this rest. Stop feeling uncomfortable about turning your home over to someone else. Lauren, you're family." Miss Wilma replied reassuringly. "You know the Ladies Auxiliary did not mind at all. They started preparing food when they learned about Sam. They all were trying to get information about Sam and to speculate on who murdered her, but I controlled that, I sent the men to the Que Shack. They can have a pissing contest without an audience."

Lauren laughed, Miss Wilma had a way with words. Feeling her head cleared from the potent migraine medication it occurred to Lauren that Miss Wilma must be feeling terrible about the murder of someone she raised from a child to adulthood.

Looking at the woman, she could tell that Sam's death was taking its toll on her. Her eyes were encased with dark circles which meant that she hadn't slept since getting the news about Sam. There were tears in those wise eyes that never fell, and every now and then her hands would tremble. Miss Wilma was doing a good job of being strong when she was a wreck just like everyone else, Lauren concluded.

"Miss Wilma, how are you really doing?" Lauren asked studying the older woman's reactions to the question.

"Oh, I'm fine. Just fine." She answered as she looked around the perfectly cleaned kitchen to find something to do to avoid this conversation.

"I don't think so. Sam and Danny are like your children instead of your nieces so, it must be hard for you to lose one to murder and have another one being stalked by the same murderer."

Then one tear rolled down her badly wrinkled cheek. Putting her fist to her forehead as if she was trying to hold back a waterfall of tears, she replied.

"It's so hard, Lauren. It's like someone pulled my heart out. I'm devastated about Sam but I can't concentrate on her death because I'm trying to keep Danny alive. I'm calling on my faith." Tears were falling faster and faster now. Lauren got some tissue from the counter and handed them to her. Wiping her face, the grieving woman continued. "I know He is with me, but I can't feel Him. I know He won't put more on me than I can bear. I know when Christians feel this way they should just stand and wait on the Lord." Her voice softened some as she continued to speak. "As you know, Jay and I couldn't have kids of our own, and then suddenly, when Gail-Ann died, God rest her soul, I had a chance to be a mother. These poor little girls didn't have a mother or a father. Edward, their father, was killed in action in Vietnam when Sam was just a year old." At this point, Miss Wilma seemed to be talking to herself. Lauren poured her some more coffee and just listened. She knew most of the story from Danny, but Miss Wilma needed to talk. It seemed odd because Miss Wilma was always in control, she was cool under pressure, and a force to be reckoned with where her family was concerned. "Here, I had Jay, who was devastated by losing his only brother and Gail-Ann was not consolable after losing her husband and the father of her children. But I held us together as best as I could with the help of the Lord. In all things Lauren, you must be strong in the Lord. But- "she slapped her hands on the counter of the kitchen island, "when Gail-Ann died, I didn't think I could make it through, but the kids needed me more. They brought me joy and happiness; oh, it was hard at first. I let them know I would never try to take their mother's place. I just wanted to love them and keep them safe but now Sam is gone, too. What am I going to do?" Then she put her head down on the island's table top and wept mournfully.

Lauren held her hand as she let her feelings out. No one had actually talked to Miss Wilma about her feelings because she was the family problem solver, the strong one. Lauren was glad she took the time to listen to her grief. In a way, Miss Wilma was just like Danny, independent and headstrong. People like them are always putting others well-being ahead of their own.

After a while, Miss Wilma wiped her face again, and looked at Lauren with sad, red eyes and said, "I am so sorry, Lauren. I am usually in control of my emotions. I guess it needed to come out. When I talk to Jay about how I feel, he always tries to make things better, and that's good, but sometimes I just need someone I trust to listen. I don't tell my business to anyone and to no one outside of this family."

"I know," Lauren said smoothly as she hugged Miss Wilma. "I'm glad to know that you consider me family.

Now, let's make some sandwiches for the men. They haven't eaten all day and who knows what is going on in the shack."

"Ain't that the truth. I wouldn't want to be out there with all of that testosterone in one place. It's a wonder Slicks got out without being murdered."

"He told me he was manhandled and threatened a few times." Miss Wilma added.

As they began to make sandwiches, Lauren asked, "Do you think Slicks hurt Sam?"

"Lord, no," Miss Wilma laughed, "He loved Baby Cakes. I believe she loved him, too. He just wouldn't leave the street life for her. It's all he's ever known. His mother, Mildred, ran the streets and partied from the day he was born. He had to fend for himself from an early age. That girl would leave him with friends and come back days later, then when he was 7 years old or so, she would leave him in the care of his brother Ace for weeks at a time. Sam met him in grade school, and she would help him with homework. I believe she would even pack extra stuff in her lunch to share with him. I made sure we had enough on hand for her to help him out, although neither of them would admit the food was for him. By middle school, he had figured out how to survive on the streets. He started hanging out with older boys who taught him how to work the streets."

"What exactly was Slicks' deal?"

"It seems that Slicks learned how to gamble with extraordinary skill. Then the skill became a habit. I guess this is how he got his name. Of course, Jay looked into Slicks when he found out that Baby Cakes was spending time with him."

"Yes, yes," Lauren laughed when she thought about how thrilled Sam was about being called Baby Cakes by Slicks.

"Yeah," Miss Wilma agreed. "The problem was when he won, he won big time money but losing caused him to be out of control. He would do anything to get a stake so he could get back in the game and win his money back. That's the part that Sam couldn't deal with in their relationship. I told her that she needed to stop taking his money. If she wouldn't be with him when he was on a losing streak, then she shouldn't be with him when he won big. Oh, this was hard for her and him but they worked it out so they could still be friends with benefits. If you know what I mean." She explained with a knowing smile. Lauren laughed agreeing that Slicks and Sam had a strange relationship. The peculiar part was that neither of them developed a serious relationship with anyone else. They dated different people, but nothing ever progressed beyond a few dates."

The conversation was interrupted when the men came through the kitchen door. It was apparent to both women that Kevin was pissed, Chief J was worried, and Anthony was bewildered.

"Lauren, I hope you don't mind if Wilma and I sleep here tonight. Danny won't wake up until in the morning, and I really don't want to get her up to take her home." The chief announced.

"I'd feel better if she were here with all of us to protect her," Anthony added.

"Sure, you and Miss Wilma can have our room, and we can sleep on the fold out," Lauren suggested as she got up to leave in order to prepare for the comfort of her guests.

"No, wait." cried Miss Wilma. "We can sleep on the fold out. I know Jay will rest better being close to Danny and you need to get some deep sleep. There are some hard times coming up for all of us."

"But I can't let…" Anthony started to protest but was cut off by The Chief.

"She's right, we'll take the fold out. This way I can be sure that she is safe."

Sulking in the corner of the kitchen, Kevin stated boldly. "I will know that she is safe because I will sleep in her room tonight." With that said Kevin promptly left the room.

"What is that all about?" Lauren asked, referring to Kevin's sullen disposition.

"I'll tell you later," Anthony said.

"That girl will make him lose his mind. Danny is the only one I know that can make him crazy." Chief J stated in a matter of fact voice.

Everyone laughed because they knew it was the truth. Danielle Elizabeth Johnston brought out the very best and the very worst in Kevin Tyler Williams.

CHAPTER SEVEN

This has been a hard day, Lauren thought as she got into the king size bed in the bedroom she shared with her husband. Lying beside him now she could see that something was troubling his mind. Anthony wasn't as intense as her brother, but when he was silent something wasn't right.

"What's going on, baby?" She asked rubbing his rock hard abs. This action could be a sign of sexual suggestion or in this case, a soothing sensation. Tonight the rubbing was a sign of soothing.

Blowing a long sigh, Anthony answered, "It's this case with Sam, Danny, and your brother."

"Oh, so he gets to be my brother now that there are problems. No, Best Partner Ever, Road Dog, or Brother- in- Law." Lauren said playfully trying to lighten his mood.

"Woman, where is your shame? I am suffering here," he laughed. Then he said, "Chief Taylor took Kevin off of the case tonight."

"What?!" Lauren questioned sitting up." Turning on her side to face her husband, she asked, "How did he take it?"

"Not well," Anthony replied. After a pause, he explained. "We were charting the possible suspects. Of course, we started with Slicks..."

Lauren interrupted him. "Slicks? Anthony, you know Slicks wouldn't hurt Sam. He loved her."

"I know, I know but honey, this case is so bizarre that we can't leave out anyone. We have to examine everyone in Sam's life so Slicks is a good place to start. Then there is the unknown Doctor who threatened her at the Drug Rehab Center." Lauren almost interrupted again, but he put up a finger and continued. "But before then, we eliminated ourselves. Chief J, Kevin and I were together when Danny went to Sam's apartment."

Lauren looked horrified. "Baby, do you think one of us killed Sam and tried to kill Danny?"

"You know how this works. You are only taken aback because, you, like your brother, are too close to the victim in this case to be objective. Step out of the picture and let's look at this situation. If you go on the premises where the person who killed Sam tried to kill Danny then we are all suspects and must be excluded by where we were when Danny was attacked."

He examined his wife's face to see if she was following his train of thought because he needed to talk this through without bias parties being present, namely his brother law, Kevin. Lauren was a furious defender of Danny, but she wasn't as in love with her as her brother.

Satisfied that Lauren understood him so far, he continued. "Ok, Chief J, Kevin and I were together when Danny was assaulted. You were at the store, that's easy to prove. Miss Wilma was at the church with the Ladies Auxiliary Committee, also easy to check. Then we came to the part that sent your brother over the edge. The people close to both Sam and Danny that don't have an alibi, and had good reasons to hurt Danny and Sam. Are you still with me?"

"Yes, but I am afraid to hear who is on that list."

By this time they were sitting up in the bed and looking at each other intensively.

Anthony went on, "Slicks is at the top of the list because we always look at the victim's love interest. He really doesn't have an alibi. Then there is Ace, Slicks' brother who was on the scene and fighting with Danny. Wes was following Danny today, and Teah is on the list because lately, she has been on this crusade to keep Kevin and

Lindsey together. She has shown some strange behavior toward Danny. What is that all about?"

"I don't know. Danny has always been protective of her because she was so behind in school. We all knew that she was a good candidate for the Special Education Program in school, but her mother wouldn't approve, so we made up for some of her short-comings. But she would say things to Danny or about Danny that were rude and not funny. Depending on her mood, Danny would sometimes fire back at her, then Teah would pull the tearful please-be-my-friend act, or say, "Girl, I was just playing with you." I just started laying into her every time she did it because I just couldn't make Danny see that Teah was jealous of her, or in my words "a back-stabbing bitch." But, 'Oh, no Lauren', Danny would say, 'We must look after people like her.' Then she continued to help her. I guess, in a way, we all did."

"She is definitely on the list. But, this is where the shit hit the fan. Lindsey. When Chief Taylor suggested Lindsey Harris Williams would be a major suspect to interview, Kevin spazzed out of control."

Lauren put her hand over her mouth as she listened to Anthony and tried to imagine just how badly Kevin reacted. He was always so laid back and sensible, and he almost never lost his temper but when he did flip out it wasn't pretty.

Lauren and Kevin came from an abusive family and at that time nobody ever talked about spousal abuse.

Their father was the manager of the Supremacy Bank of Louisville. Looking back, this was a very prestigious job, a black man as the overseer of a bank. This position added much respect to their family name. Lance Williams' family had everything they needed and more. However, there was a different side to Lance Williams that no one saw but his wife, Sara Williams. Secretly, Lance had been abusing Sara. No one knew because Sara, his wife of twenty years, always pretended that she had the "perfect family" and she would do anything to keep it that way. However, their sixteen-year-old son, Kevin Williams had become suspicious when he began to notice bruises on his mother's upper arms as she moved around the lovely home that was provided by her loving husband. Sara Williams didn't work outside the house as other women had started to do during that time, because her husband earned a good income. She was the homemaker for her family, but Kevin suspected that something else was going on, so he started his first investigation.

He watched for patterns in his parent's relationship, good days at the bank often brought flowers, wine or surprise gifts from their father to their mother. Bad days were very tense.

Once he saw his mother tremble when she heard the car door of Lance's 1981 Buick Riviera slam shut.

On that particular day Lauren, Danny, Teah, and Lindsey were at their middle school's cheerleader tryouts, and Kevin announced to his parents that he and Anthony had football practice at Shawnee Park.

But Kevin didn't leave the house. Instead, he hid in the basement right under his mother and father's bedroom. He could hear his father pacing about and Kevin knew that pacing meant his father was upset.

Sara Williams came into the bedroom, "Honey, can I get you an iced tea?"

"No, "his father answered, "but you can explain to me why we are late on this month's Visa credit card."

"Oh, Lance," Sara cried with fear in her voice, for she knew what was coming next, "I totally forgot. Lauren has been sick with the flu. I had to take her to the doctor--."

She was interrupted by a blow to the face.

The sound of his father's hands hitting his mother erupted a rage in Kevin that he had never felt before in his life. He raced up the steps and entered his parent's bedroom. It seemed like time froze for him, or like he was another person, his father had pushed a shaking Sara onto the bed where he was slapping her back and forth across her face. Seeing his father knocking around his mother enraged Kevin even more.

He snatched Lance Williams away from his mother and proceeded to beat him senseless. While he was beating his dad, Sara was screaming for Kevin to stop, because she feared that Kevin would beat him to death. The older man didn't have a chance to defend himself, so he cowered down in the corner of the room, and hoped that Kevin soon came to his senses.

His mother was a member of Ephesians Baptist Church's Ladies Auxiliary, and Miss Wilma stopped by the Williams' home to drop off some flyers for the group's next fundraiser for the church. When she heard the screaming, she dropped the packages of flyers and ran into the house. When she got to the bedroom, she saw Kevin beating his father to a bloody pulp, while Sara with swelling bruises on her face, was trying to get between her son and husband. But Sara was not getting anywhere trying to deter her son from the horrific beating he was giving her husband.

However, Miss Wilma had a commanding voice, and she used that voice to quickly put an end to the savage thrashing Kevin was giving his father.

"Kevin Tyler Williams! You stop this nonsense at once! Come here, Kevin!" the short woman commanded.

Her voice cut through to the sane part of his mind, and he dropped his dad to the floor and went to Miss Wilma hugging her and crying. "He was hurting my mom! He was hurting her!"

That was what Lauren heard when she got to the driveway of their home. She saw the police and an ambulance were parked in front in the driveway, but they wouldn't let her and Danny enter the house where the crying and other loud voices were coming out of the window of their parent's bedroom. She and Danny huddle together looking like two scared kittens.

Lauren remembered her whole body bracing for something awful to be revealed to her, but Miss Wilma came out of the house to tell her that everything was going to be alright and that she and Danny needed to leave with her. Both girls went with her without a word. When Miss Wilma handled a situation there were little questions to be asked because everyone just followed her directions.

Looking back, she remembered how upset Kevin was that day and she had never seen him that upset before. She hoped that Anthony's description of "spazzed out" didn't mean that he actually went there, as he did on the last day she ever saw her father. Soon after that day, her father quickly divorced their mother, left town and never returned.

"Lauren, are you with me?" Anthony asked after noticing that she had drifted for a minute or two.

Giving herself a quick mental shake, because the memory of that day still devastated her emotional being to the core. She was glad to get back to the present. She asked, "What happened?"

Anthony continued telling the events of the shack. "Chief Taylor asked about Lindsey's whereabouts when Danny was attacked, and immediately Kevin became defensive. He claimed that it couldn't be Lindsey because she wasn't that kind of person. Then Chief Taylor asked him about his relationship with Danny and Lindsey. Kevin answered him by saying it was none of his business. Long story short, Lindsey's name was added to the list of suspects, and Kevin is on a mandated leave of absence."

"Oh," she gasped. "Well, at least the Chief didn't fire him. So, what about her motive and alibi?"

"Her motive? One word, Kevin. We have to check out her schedule of events for today."

"What a mess. So, who do you think did this?"

"I don't know. All of the people on the list have very real motives for hurting Sam and Danny.

"Not Lindsey. I can see her hurting Danny, but Sam?"

"Yeah? So ask yourself this, who knew that sweet little Lindsey was in love with Kevin all these years, or how she planned to take him away from Danny? I don't put anything past her. She could have killed Sam just to get Danny to come home, so she could off her for good."

He sighed and laid back down on the bed, pulling Lauren with him, "I'm sorry, baby for unloading on you like this, but my partner has his hands full with trying to solve Sam's murder, trying to keep Danny alive, and dealing with his conniving wife. I won't even mention that Chief J is silently putting the screws to him about Danny."

"*Wow!* That's a lot. I wish I could help him. I hope he can hold himself together."

"So do I. But if Kevin is dealing with Lindsey and Danny, how can he get his head on straight? Maybe this leave is what he needs to handle his business."

"How is he going to solve Sam's murder if he's not allowed to work on her case?"

"Ha!" Anthony Laughed, "You know what that leave means. It means that he is free to investigate this murder as he sees fit, and he will. We both know that is what he will do."

"What if it is Lindsey?"

"Hey! Let's not tempt fate. One shit at a time."

They both were silent for a moment, each processing what they had discussed. After a while, Lauren said, "Well, I kind of like being your partner in crime. Feel better?"

"I do, but you can continue to sooth me in this, my hour of need."

Lauren giggled and continued to rub his rock hard abs, however, soothing was not the target this time.

CHAPTER EIGHT

In the guestroom, Kevin turned back the covers to get into bed with Danny but before getting into the bed, he took a moment just to look at her. He hadn't been able to just look at her for 4 years. She looked gorgeous just lying there peacefully sleeping. Her long, black hair fanned out on the pillows like black silk ribbons. He closed his eyes to remember how it felt to touch it and how it smelled when he held her. As his eyes moved down her body, he felt a stirring in his soul. He looked at her curves and lastly, he embraced the sight of her long, perfectly shaped, slender legs. Being a B and L man, this was the woman for him. However, he loved her for her innocent spirit. She had heart and soul for everything and everybody.

Then pain entered his time of peace for he recognized that his one night of sin with her best friend had ended their relationship. Sitting on the side of the bed with his hand covering his face, he just couldn't imagine a life without Danny but that 5'6, 110 pound woman was a force to be reckoned with once she felt betrayed. Danny never had a gray area in her evaluation of occurrences in life that hurt her. It was either black or white, you did, or you didn't. She didn't believe in variables, circumstances, or basically excuses. A person's actions were executed for the desired outcomes, whatever they may be. She thought that he had slept with her best friend because in her words, he was a horny dog that couldn't be trusted.

Laying down he prayed, "Lord, please give me strength to change her mind." Kevin knew she still loved him; his job was to get pass that wall of distrust. With Sam's death and someone trying to kill her, where the hell was he going to start trying to rebuild their relationship?

Sighing, he laid down beside her and instantly, in her drug induced state, she whispered, "Kevin."

Shocked, he rose up to look at her she was half asleep. "I'm here. Go back to sleep, baby."

She looked at him in her dazed state and questioned, "Are you really here with me?"

"Yes, come here," He said pulling her into his arms.

She let out a sigh of relief and rested her head on his chest and said in a very relaxed and confused voice, "I've called you every night, but you never come."

So, she does think about me, he mused as he assured her that he was really there.

Then she went back to sleep with those long legs curled around his body. "Oh, yeah!" His soul sang. There was hope for getting what he loved most back in his life.

Tonight he couldn't help but be "a horny dog" with those legs wrapped around his body what was a man supposed to think about. This is going to be a long, agonizing night, but this is where he wanted to be even if it is just for one night.

Later that night, he woke up to hands exploring his body. Danny, still in her state of twilight, was seducing him, and it was working. He turned toward her, and they shared a long passionate kiss. Using all of the will power he had, he pulled away from her.

"Danny!" He whispered in desperation, "We can't do this!"

Whining in protest, she asked, "Why?"

"Because, baby, you are not yourself right now. Look at me, Danny. Oh, I want you but not like this. When we make love again, and we will, I want you to be in your right mind not drugged out. I don't want you to have regrets in the morning. I promise that we will be together soon."

"You promise?" she asked already laying down on his shoulder again. She was asleep before she could hear him say, "You can count on it."

That was close, Kevin thought, rubbing Danny's arms. At least he was able to stop that train before it became a wreck. Unlike the last time, he should have stopped but didn't use the will power. He replayed that awful night that stole his life forever. If only he had listened to his big head and not the little one then he would be in a better place. As the story played in his head, he tried to find some justification for his actions, but he couldn't find any.

He had just started the police academy, and the training was extensive. Danny was studying for the 8-hour Teacher Specialty test, so there wasn't too much time to spare to spend with each other.

But time waits for no one, and it was spring in Kentucky again. It was time for a fresh beginning and a feeling of new hope for the future. It was also time for the Spring Fling Thing sponsored once again by the Johnston's at Masonic Hall. It seemed that each year the dance got larger and more prestigious. This year Kevin wanted to go and spend some time with Danny, because they had been so occupied with career business that they hadn't seen much of each other. But when he asked her to go to the dance with him on the coming Saturday, she declined because she had to study for an 8-hour test which was scheduled for Monday.

Kevin was angry and disappointed when Danny turned down his invitation to go to the dance with him.

"Come on, Dan!" He begged. "We haven't been anywhere for months."

Looking at her notes and not really looking at him she said, "I know, but the big test is scheduled for Monday, and I have to pass it."

"But we always go-," He started to say, but they were interrupted by the doorbell. Kevin opened the door because Danny didn't seem to hear it. Then Lauren, Teah, Sam, and Lindsey rushed into the house. The talk turned to who was going to the dance with whom. Lauren was going with Anthony, Teah was going with Ace, Sam was going with Slicks, but Lindsey didn't have a date.

Danny was half listening to the girls as she was still studying.

"Dan! Are you listening?" Teah asked, "We all need to go to the dance together. Ace is renting a limo so we can ride together and party as hard as we want."

"Ah," Danny moaned, "sounds like fun but I can't go."

"What!?" They all shouted.

Frowning at her friends Danny explained, "I've got a big test Monday. Unc paid big money for me to take this test so, I can't fail. I've got to study."

The girls all groaned, and then Sam protested, "Dan, you always study too hard. You know you'll pass this test. Come on, don't miss this fun."

"No. There are a couple of areas that I am weak in, and I have to build them up. I'm sorry."

"I've been begging her already with no luck," Kevin said, sadly.

"Please try to understand. There will be another dance next year, but I need to pass this test on Monday."

"Okay," Teah said, "then Kevin can take Lindsey so, she'll have a date."

"What?!" Exclaimed Sam and Lauren.

"Hey, it will be a friendship date, nothing special. Danny, I know he's your man so it will be like sister and brother. Is it alright?" Lindsey said assuredly, trying to clear up any misunderstanding.

Danny was still distracted by this conversation and what direction her study session should take.

"If it's ok with Kevin then it is okay with me," Danny said at last.

Everyone looked at Kevin, one-half of the group, Lauren and Sam wanted him to say no, and the other half, Teah, and Lindsey wanted him to say yes.

"Okay, only if it's okay with you." Kevin finally said.

"I'm okay with this," giving him a kiss, "I trust you."

If Kevin's imaginary train had stopped right then, he would be a happier man today.

Well, it didn't stop, in fact, the train that was on the wrong track picked up speed. He and Lindsey missed the Limo ride with the others because Lindsey was still at the beauty salon getting her hair fixed. She explained that the stylist ran late due to the number of women who were trying to get a last minute hairdo for the important dance. When Lindsey called Kevin to let him know that they would miss the limo ride with their friends, he had to run out to the nearest car service to get his Black 1990 Lincoln Continental Mark VII washed and detailed.

He called Danny before he went to pick up Lindsey. She was into her studies and hurried him off the phone, and he was pissed off by this action. It was bad enough that she wasn't going to the dance with him, loaned him out to her friend like he was a bowl of sugar that the next door neighbor needed, and then she didn't even want to be bothered by his disappointment. He was heated, and his last thoughts as he left his house were to hell with Danny and her damned test.

He was still fuming when he pulled in front of Lindsey's house, but that feeling didn't last long. When Lindsey stepped out of the door, his eyes nearly popped out of his head. She was wearing a form fitting red dress that showed off all of her curves. The neckline descended to the middle chest so the front of the dress barely covered her small but firm breasts. Two thin straps held the front of the dress in place while crossing in the lower part of her back. The hem of the dress stopped just below her well-formed butt and there was a zipper that went from the lower part of her back to the end of the dress. Her shapely legs were showing from her upper thighs to the very high and ravishing red ankle strapped shoes. His eyes went to her face. Every minute in the salon was well worth it. Her makeup was perfect, and all of her naturally curly hair was pulled to one side.

Turning around in the driveway she asked, "You like?"

He scrambled out of the Lincoln to open the door for her, bending down to get the door handle he could smell her expensive perfume. "Yes, I do." He managed to say. "You look gorgeous."

As she got into the spacious car, her legs parted just enough to make him wonder if she was wearing any panties.

It was getting dark, and he had to get her to the dance where other people would be around to help keep his mind off of what he wanted to do to her.

When they got to Masonic Hall's Parking lot it was full so he had to go to the back of the lot to park.

When he turned off the car, Lindsey started to cry.

"What is wrong, Lin?" Kevin asked with concern scooting close to her.

"I don't think I can go in," she sniffed.

"Why? You look beautiful."

"Well, Sam and Lauren don't really like me, and I just feel funny being with you."

"Hey, it's just a dance and we are friends so, let's just show them how wrong they are. Come on, let's just go in."

Then she actually started to cry, "I'm scared, Kevin. I don't want to lose my friends."

He pulled her into his arms to comfort her but when she looked up at him with those amazing big brown eyes screaming with lust, he lost all control, and she did not stop him. The first passionate kiss led to another, and then he found himself un-zipping the back of the dress which came off in his hands and to add to his lust, she was only wearing the dress, no bra, and no panties just bright red strappy shoes.

They rumpled in the backseat of the Lincoln until the dance was nearly over. He couldn't get enough of her, and she couldn't get enough of him.

Then it happened, the realization of what they were doing set in like a slap in the face. The consequences of their actions were screaming at him.

"What the hell are we doing?" Kevin asked desperately.

"Oh, Kevin. This got out of hand. What are we going to do?"

Putting his clothes back on, he answered, "I don't know."

She was putting the only piece of clothing she wore that night back on when it hit him.

He looked at the real Lindsey for the first time that evening and said, "You set me up!"

Vindictively she said, "And you liked it."

"You bitch!"

Waving one finger at him she replied, "Sorry honey, but that ain't what you called me a while ago."

Sliding into the front seat, Lindsey pulled down the mirror on the car's sun visor and began to repair her make-up.

Turning around in the seat she said, "Oh, Kevin look, it was just a roll in the hay. No one has to know about it. It will be just between you and me. We'll tell the others that we just didn't go to the dance."

Feeling a sense of relief, he agreed. Starting the Lincoln he took her home and didn't look at her when she got out of the car. Kevin drove home as fast as he could to wash her off of him. After he had showered, he went to see Danny who was still studying. After kissing her, Kevin grabbed a book and started grilling her on its content. He hoped that his night of sin would not come back to bite him in the ass but that dream didn't last long.

His mind wouldn't let him continue with the thoughts of the past, so he pulled a snoring Danny into spoon with him.

"Danny, I hope you can hear me. I am sorry for ruining our lives. Promise me that you will not leave Kentucky without talking to me, just you and me alone. Promise, please?" He sobbed into the back of her hair.

To his surprise, she answered, "I promise."

CHAPTER NINE

Her answer both surprised him and worried him. Could she just be saying this in her sleep, or did she really understand what he was asking? Whatever the deal, he thought, she had promised to talk to him before she went back to California. A feeling of contentment filled his soul, and he fell asleep with the woman that he loved and had lost in his arms.

The next morning at eight o' clock, Miss Wilma knocked on the door of the guest room to wake Danny and Kevin for breakfast.

Waking up in Kevin's arms was a bit confusing, and then it all came rushing back to her that someone had tried to kill her. She looked over at Kevin and thought, where else would he be? She knew he loved her, but there was too much baggage to pick through for them to ever be together.

She kissed him gratefully and said, "Thank you, Kevin, for being with me last night."

"I will always be here for you, anywhere you need me." Then he hugged her.

"We'd better hurry, Anthony and some homicide detectives will be here at ten to interview you about what happened yesterday. I am officially off of this case because of our history, but if you want me to be there when they talk to you then you have to tell them. I know Chief Johnston will be there as "family," but I want to be in there when they question you."

"Kevin, I want you to investigate this case. You know...knew Sam, you can see things that strangers can't."

"I know you do, and I was upset when they decided that I was too close to the case to be objective, but I can work this to our advantage. I can protect you and do my own investigation at the same time. I am sure that Chief Johnston is not going to just stand by and do nothing. Just trust me, Danny, this will work out."

"Ok. You know what you're doing." Danny slipped out of the bed and padded barefoot to the bathroom door, she heard Lauren's voice in her head saying, "face this and fix it one way or another." So, she looked back at him and said, "No matter what, I promise not to leave Kentucky without talking to you."

"You heard me?" Kevin asked feeling a sense of comfort.

"Yes, I did but that is all I promise. I will listen, and that is all."

"That is all I want." He said, hopefully. Suddenly feeling that the light at the end of the tunnel had just come back on again, he thought, "Just maybe I have a shot at the one thing I loved in life."

Miss Wilma and Lauren were busy cooking and preparing a huge country breakfast. The menu consisted of eggs, sausage, fried chicken, gravy, biscuits, hash brown potatoes, oatmeal, tomatoes, cucumbers, grapes, melons and home-made preserves. Of course, there was a prayer, led by Chief Johnston which included a request for Danny's protection from harm. The food was delicious, but Danny just couldn't eat much of it. Miss Wilma insisted that she eat the fruits and vegetables.

Promptly, at 10 o'clock the detectives arrived at the house. Detectives Hale, Hickman, and Wilson would be interviewing Danny today. For the privacy of this meeting, Miss Wilma suggested that they interview Danny in the Que Shack where they wouldn't be interrupted by visitors and other interested people. Everyone agreed that this was a good idea but before they left for the shack Danny said, "Anthony, I need Kevin to stay with me during this interview."

"Sweetie, Kevin is not working this case," Anthony informed her, giving Kevin the I-know-what-you're-doing eye.

"He told me, but I'd feel better if he was with me."

"Ok," Anthony agreed, then said to Kevin, "You have no input in this interview, no matter what is said. You know that."

Kevin just nodded, creeping back into his dark and mysterious disposition.

No one questioned whether Chief J was going to the interview so, everyone left for the shack at the back of the house.

Once inside, Kevin noticed the white boards that were filled with the suspect's names and motives were covered up. The screen that Anthony used to show vacations slides and videos was now used to conceal the board's information about the case. In Anthony's shack there was a large pool table, so everyone pulled up a chair. Chief J, Danny, and Kevin were on one side of the table, and Detectives Hickman, Wilson, and Hale were on the other side.

After the introductions had been given and Kevin was reminded that he was only there to support the victim then the questioning started.

"I am sorry for your loss and the attack on your life yesterday," Hale said looking directly at Danny.

She acknowledged his condolences for her sister and his apology for her horrendous experience yesterday by just nodding.

"The purpose of this meeting is to gather information to help us further investigate these dreadful, and evil crimes which have deeply affected you and your family. We will make records of what is said here today by the use of recording and written notes so we can refer to them with complete accuracy. Also, we want to be able to contact you for clarifications from time to time so, at the end of this interview we would like for you to leave us your contact numbers."

"We understand that most of these procedures are familiar to you because of your Uncle's superb job with the LPD but if there is something that you don't understand just stop us so we can explain."

Hale turned on the recorder and Hickman took out a pad and an ink pen.

"Let's get started. It was reported to us that on April 5th you went to your sister's apartment at 4530 West Broadway about 5:00 p.m. Take it from there and slowly tell us what happened. Start from the time you opened the door to Samantha Johnston's apartment."

Bravely, Danny told them about walking through the apartment looking at pictures that Sam had on the walls and end tables. She described how she went to the safe to get the insurance papers when she saw the person running toward her.

"Wait." Detective Hale interrupted, "Describe that person."

"I really couldn't tell whether it was a man or a woman," Danny said trying to think back without the horror affecting her ability to see the person. "Let's see, the intruder was wearing a purple wool scarf around its neck and green army fatigues. It was wearing black gloves with the fingers cut out and it had a large knife in its right hand."

"Ok, let's take it back." Detective Hickman stopped her. "Try to remember the type of knife that the attacker had."

"It was big and shiny," then she remembered where she had seen a knife like the one the killer had been holding in their hands. "It was like the knife my daddy had, it was an army knife. I remember seeing pictures of him with an army knife."

"Her father, Captain Edward Johnston, was a member of the United States Army. He was killed in the Vietnam War, so she would be familiar with his equipment." Chief Johnston interjected.

"This is good to know," Hale said making a note of this detail.

"Ok, so you said the intruder was wearing army fatigues, do you know from what era?"

"No but they weren't from Desert Storm." Danny said thinking hard about where she had seen these fatigues. Then she remembered the picture of her father in a green army uniform. Looking at Chief J she said, "It was wearing fatigues like Daddy used to wear."

"Was it from the Vietnam era, Danny, just green?" Chief J asked.

"Yes, all dull green but there were no tags or ranks on them." She answered.

"Is anyone in the family active in the military?" Wilson asked.

"Not at this time. My brother was the only one in the family who was military." Chief Johnston replied.

"Now," Detective Hale said, "You stated that the gloves had the fingers cut out. Could you tell if they were a man's fingers or the race of the attacker?"

Danny thought back to the moment she saw the attacker's hands and said, "The race was African-American, but I couldn't tell if the fingers were of a male or female, I'm sorry."

"No, you're doing just great. Did the person speak to you?" Hickman asked.

"Yes, but the voice seemed to sound like a robot or something like that. It said, "I was going to take my time with you, but since you are here, I'll have to make this quick." Then it started across the bed, and I shot it center mass three times." Danny's voice began to elevate because she was getting upset again.

Kevin leaned over and whispered in her ear "Calm down, baby. You are not there; you are just remembering. I won't let anything happen to you."

Hearing his reassuring voice, her breathing returned to normal.

"Do you need a break?" Chief Johnston asked.

"No, I'm okay." Pausing to gather her thoughts she continued, "I was surprised to see the creature running outside the apartment, then stopping at the kitchen window it said, "This ain't over bitch!" I can still see its masked face. It looked like a character from the Night of the Living Dead. It was a full head mask. Again, I couldn't tell if it was a man or a woman." She thought for a second then asked, "If the freak was outside threatening me, then who was I fighting with in the kitchen?"

"It was a Victor Malone." Detective Hale answered looking through some notes that he'd taken earlier. "I believe you call him Ace. We've gotten his statement already. It seems that he was trying to protect you, but you attacked him."

"Oh no, Ace! Is he alright? Danny exclaimed. "I didn't know it was him."

"He's okay. He is being released this afternoon." Anthony replied. "He understands."

"Did you want to add anything else?"

"It happened so fast, that's all I can remember. I fired at the creature two more times through the kitchen window. I know that I hit it both times so, why didn't it die or stay down?"

"It probably was wearing a bullet proof vest."

"Do you know of anyone who would want to hurt you?"

"No, not right off. I haven't lived here for 4 years."

"Any conflicts that you can remember having with anyone before you left Louisville?" Detective Wilson asked.

She looked at Kevin while her heart felt like it was being squeezed by vice-grips.

"Yes," She painfully replied.

"Tell us about it." Detective Hickman requested with great interest.

"I can't!" Danny said with strained intensity.

Seeing that she was getting very upset, Detective Hale changed the interviewing strategy.

"Ok, from our short investigation, we've learned that there are some unresolved and serious problems between you, Lindsey Harris Williams, and Detective Kevin Williams."

"That's true."

"We have eliminated Detective Williams because the three of them, Detectives Porter, Williams and Chief Johnston were together when this attack took place."

"But according to our notes, Mrs. Lindsey Williams has good reasons to want you, well, not here."

"Why would she kill Sam?" Danny asked.

"Maybe to get you to come home. We are working on many motives and suspects so, you need to stay safe. Do not go anywhere alone for the time being."

The meeting ended and Danny felt a great sense of relief. As she and Kevin walked back to the house she was in deep thought which caused Kevin to be concerned.

"Danny, remember the promise, please."

"I do but this is so painful; you, Lindsey, and the baby. I can hardly breathe."

She walked ahead of him to the house. When she went inside, there were people throughout the house expressing their condolences with words, cards, and food. There were about fifteen people, some doctors, and nurses from Sam's job and church members.

A tearful co-worker of Sam's stopped Danny when she walked in and started to tell her how sorry she was about Sam's death and how she was going to miss her when they were interrupted by the booming voice of Teah. Holding the living room's landline in her hand she announced loudly across the room, "Kevin, your wife is on the phone."

The whole room froze, and then everyone turned to look at Danny. Quickly, Kevin walked toward the phone and Chief J stepped close to Danny. As Kevin put the phone to his ear, Danny sent him a look that would instantly curdle milk. Her eyes were sending him degrees of sizzling hate.

Chief lifted her chin and whispered, "Pack a bag. You're spending the day at home. Where there are no well-wishers. You need to rest. Let's go."

Danny turned toward the guest room where she had spent the night with Kevin, and now she was packing to get rid of him. Her protective fog was returning, it was a welcomed rescue because to think now would tear her apart.

She was slowly packing a bag when Lauren came into the room to help. Silently, they packed a small bag for the stay at Uncle J and Aunt Wilma's house or, in other words, home.

CHAPTER TEN

Chief J was talking quietly to Miss Wilma when Danny and Lauren came out of the bedroom. They both looked concerned as they seemed to come to an agreement.

Scanning the room, it seemed like more people were in the house, and this was too much for Danny. How could she smile and be a strong mourner when her heart was breaking from death and betrayal? Deep down, she knew that most of the people knew the situation between herself, Lindsey and Kevin and with Sam's murder some were here just to get extra gossip. Up to now, she had put on a pleasant face and an I-don't-care attitude, but she didn't have the strength for that performance today.

She hated herself for doing it, but she looked around the room for Kevin. He wasn't in there. She hated herself even more when she thought that he had gone home to Lindsey. More pain, physical, unbearable pain was causing her to experience some spasm-like sensations throughout her entire body. It took all of her strength to anchor herself to the floor. Standing there looking at all of the supporters and information seekers caused her hands to start trembling.

"No! No! No," her brain screamed. "No one can see you like this. Where is the fog?!"

Saving her from total disgrace and gossip, her uncle appeared and asked, "Ready?"

Taking her bag and not waiting for a reply, he guided her to the kitchen where they exited the house through the back door to avoid everyone.

Louisville's Derby festival atmosphere was lost on Danny as Uncle J drove his 1994 dark teal colored Cadillac Sedan Deville around the Parkway. Thankfully, the fog had come back to save her from a complete breakdown, but she knew it was just a matter of time before the fog would become ineffective. However, at this moment she would give into it just so she would not feel the pain in her life.

The Johnstons brought up Sam and Danny in a beautiful, peaceful neighborhood. The house was located off of Southwestern Parkway on 47th Street. She and her sister would get teased for living in the Ohio River, which was almost correct. The backyard led to the river which provided some great outdoor adventures for the sisters. The two-story house was big and breezy, with a porch that almost surrounded it. The Cape Cod style house had colorful bushes and flowers on each side of the wide steps leading to the designer entry-way door. Auntie ran a well-ordered house, Danny thought as she entered the home where she grew up. Tears filled her eyes as the good feeling of being home consumed her. Here she could be herself without being judged. She didn't have to pretend that she was alright because the house seemed to say, 'welcome home, I will comfort you.'

Taking her overnight bag to the room she'd grown up in stirred up more memories. More memories of her and Kevin! Sitting on the bed, she felt her heart sink to her stomach. How can I begin to heal when he is everywhere in my life?! She agonizingly thought. She sat on her bed and started to cry. She felt like this nightmare went on and on and got worse and worse. What made her cry harder were these thoughts. Why was this happening to her? What did she do to deserve this hell on earth?

Downstairs Uncle J felt helpless hearing the niece that he and Wilma had reared crying her heart out. Sam and Danny were just like their own children. When Edward, their dad, and his only brother had been killed in Vietnam, he nearly died too. He and Wilma supported Gail-Ann through the grief and devastation of losing her husband and the father of her children. It took a long time for her to start living again. Tears started filling his eyes as he reflected on the family's tragic history. He remembered with full details the day Danny had called him crying hysterically to tell him that their mom was lying at the bottom of the basement steps not moving.

The thought of the phone call was too painful to think about, so he walked through the living room to his den where he opened the small half barreled shaped liquor cabinet and got out his favorite whiskey, Makers Mark. He filled a shot glass with the rich brown liquid and drank it straight down. The heat of the bourbon flowed down his throat, giving him a much needed smooth, warm feeling in his body and mind.

Setting out another glass, he thought, I am putting an end to some of this nonsense, starting with my willful niece.

"Danny," he called upstairs as he had done on many occasions. Like her father, Ed, she was a headstrong and unmovable person. When her mind was made up, nothing or no one could change it, but him and most of the time he picked his battles with her, but today the fight was on.

"Unc, I just want to be alone,"

"Not today. Either you come down, or I will come up." No answer came from upstairs, only the shifting of covers and feet on the steps.

Entering into the den, Unc observed that she was a mess. Her face was swollen from crying, her eyes were red with water still in them that threatened to fall in a minute, and her hair was in full disarray. He couldn't even describe the frock that she was wearing. This was not his niece, she was beautiful all the time. On the rare occasions that she did cry, no one could really tell that she was actually crying because it was done so gracefully. He hadn't seen her in this condition since her mother died. Her whole body seemed to shake as she sat on the love seat.

Handing her the shot glass of Makers Mark he said, "Down it."

When she did, he poured them another. He didn't have to tell her to down this one because she did it on her own. Setting the glasses aside, he said, "Let's talk."

"I don't want ..." Danny started to protest, but then he cut her off.

"But we're going to talk. We've got two situations going on here that are tearing you apart, and I can't let that happen."

"What can I do?" she asked looking at him with a hopeless expression.

"Danny, things are hard for you because you see things in black or white. There are no gray areas for you in any situation." She was puzzled by his observation, for he had said that to her all of her life and she never really understood why.

"Life is not like that, Dan. There are no absolute good or evil people. There may be more good in some people or more bad in some individuals, but not absolute good or bad. Take the situation between you and Kevin; you don't know what happened between Kevin and Lindsey?"

This struck a nerve, "What happened?" She shouted. "I don't need glasses to figure that out."

"Okay. Here is the black and white situation. Kevin and Lindsey slept together, she got pregnant, and they got married. Here is the gray area that you don't know, why did they have sex? Was it a one-time thing? Was it an affair? Does Kevin still want his wife? Do you know any of that? No, you just want it to go away because it is not white. You must talk to Kevin and work this out because it is eating you alive and I can't watch."

Meekly, she said, "I promised Kevin that I wouldn't leave without talking to him first but, I …"

"Danielle, you have to work this out no matter how badly it hurts then you can move on with your life. I know that there has not been anyone special in your life since Kevin. Therefore, I can only conclude that you are still in love with him." Whenever Uncle J called her Danielle she knew that he meant business.

"I want to stop being in love with him," she replied angrily.

Sitting in his favorite easy chair across from her he said,

"It doesn't work like that, Danielle. The heart wants what the heart wants, and your heart wants him no matter how hard you fight against it, mainly because you don't know the whole story. You are either going to end it with him and move on with your life, or you are going to see if the both of you can salvage this relationship."

"Please understand this, good people make poor choices because no one is perfect. I am sure that you have done some things that you are not proud of that doesn't mean that you are all bad. All humans make mistakes, but we can't forget the good that they have done and just dwell on their weaknesses. "

"Did Kevin ask you to talk to me?"

"No and I wouldn't have if he had asked. This is his problem. I just want you to be open to other colors in a situation."

"I don't want to be hurt again."

"That's not our call. You know where your strength comes from, draw on it. But today, I want you to prioritize on these unpleasant difficulties. There is Sam's murder, the funeral, the threat to your life; I will control that problem, but the Kevin and Lindsey situation is where your head should be now. Deal with these issues one at a time and stop running from them." She was quiet, so he knew that she was processing his words.

"Now, Miss Universe, have you forgotten your looks? You haven't looked like yourself since you've been home."

She gasped when she looked at herself in the large oval mirror on the wall in front of her.

"Now, let's get upstairs and repair your nails, hair and whatever else you women use to drive us men crazy and above all, burn whatever that is you're wearing."

When he saw a bright smile cross her face, then he knew he had gotten through to her. He kissed her forehead before she scurried upstairs to reinvent Danielle Elizabeth Johnston.

CHAPTER ELEVEN

April in Kentucky can be a sampling of all weather conditions, and the day of the funeral was no different. Clouds covered the sky until time for the services. Then the sun shone brightly bouncing off the black funeral cars in front of the church.

Lauren was at Ephesians Baptist Church early to play hostess until the family arrived. Along with the funeral director and staff, the police were in the church as well. After double checking everything, Lauren walked into the sanctuary to find Teah standing at Sam's closed casket sobbing uncontrollably. As she approached Teah, she noticed the many flowers and plants that were sent to honor Sam. The floral fragrance filled the church. On the book signing stand there were condolence cards and notes. Lauren was sure that Miss Wilma had someone to take care of the cards and the flowers.

Lauren approached Teah to comfort her, but she turned away from her saying, "Get away from me! You never liked me, but Sam did, and now she's gone!" Slumping her shoulders inward, she continued crying noisily. Nearby Officers looked into the room to see what was happening, but Lauren waved them off.

"Come on, Teah," Lauren said like she was soothing a child, "let's get some tissue for your face."

So, Teah went with Lauren to the ladies room. After Lauren had helped her to repair her makeup, she said, "I want you to stop this crusade against Danny."

Stunned, Teah said, "What?"

"You know what. I asked you to leave Danny alone twice, but you seem to want to continue to hurt her. This situation between Danny and my brother is not your concern. I believe that Lindsey put you up to this."

"Lindsey just wants to keep her husband. She told me that if we could keep Danny out of the picture things between her and Kevin would work out. She needs my help." Teah explained. She was looking at Lauren with a "you-know-what-I-mean" expression.

It was Lauren's turn to be stunned. She was stunned by Teah's ignorance. At last, she could see why Danny always protected her.

"Lindsey was using you, Teah. Why would you want to hurt somebody that always looked out for you? Danny was always on your side, and she never let anyone hurt you. She taught you things about life that you didn't know, and this is what you do to her? She only wants to help you."

"Help me!" Teah snapped, "All that bitch did was tell me how my man tried to screw all of us. Danny said that Ace was not right for me and that I should stay away from him. I love Ace and he ain't wrong. Danny should stay out of *my* business!"

Seeing that she could not get through to Teah, Lauren countered, "Okay. Let me put this to you another way. Remember when you got locked up for smoking marijuana with Wes and you went to jail?"

She waited for Teah to recall the incident, and then she continued, "That was scary for you, wasn't it? We helped you out of that trouble, didn't we, me and Danny?"

The thought of going back to lock up really frightened Teah. She didn't fully understand the law, but she never wanted to be put inside a holding cell ever again.

"Yes, y'all had my back. We were close friends then." She reflected.

"Now, listen to me carefully. If you do one more thing to Danny, I will have you arrested."

Teah jumped back from Lauren as if she had slapped her, "No, you can't do that, Lauren."

"Yes, I can Teah, I am married to a policeman. Just keep doing all the things Lindsey asked you to do to Danny and you will go behind bars because it's not right what you are doing to her. You think about all the many things Danny has helped you with and then think about how Lindsey will get you put in jail."

"But I was just..." The trembling Teah tried to explain, but Lauren interrupted.

"I won't tell you again, I will just have you arrested." Then Lauren walked out of the bathroom leaving Teah to process what had just happened.

Due to the crime and the attempt on Danny, the visitation and the funeral were held on the same day. People were filling the sanctuary for the visitation, but the family had not arrived at the church, so Lauren continued to greet the mourners.

Lindsey Williams stepped into the church and pranced down the aisle to sign the guestbook, there, in her best handwriting she wrote: "Sorry for your loss, Mr. and Mrs. Kevin Williams." She was in a little black dress for women who had other things on their minds, but not bereavement. She had purposely worn the red strapped heels from the famous night that she seduced Kevin. She just wanted him to remember how badly he had wanted her that night. Looking around the room, she locked eyes with another bitch friend. She waved at Lauren sweetly knowing she would have to play nice until her plans worked out. She was looking for her partner in crime, Teah. When Lindsey spotted her, Teah wouldn't make eye contact with her. What the hell was wrong with that dumb bitch now? Lindsey thought, walking toward the back of the church where Teah was sitting, but when Teah saw Lindsey walking in her direction, she left the sanctuary. Lindsey stood in the aisle watching Teah scurry away like a deformed rat. Bewildered, she took a seat next to an older couple and tried to understand what just happened. Lindsey wondered why Teah was acting so strangely because she needed that fool to complete the next phase of her plan. All the idiot had to do was get Danny alone so she could make her go away permanently but Teah was nowhere to be found.

Turning around she felt the older man next to her outwardly admiring her legs and shoes. Well, Lindsey thought, if my efforts in dressing today can turn on a dead man, there's hope that I can turn on the only man that I've ever wanted, my husband. Smiling sweetly at the older gentleman, Lindsey pretended to read the program.

After a while, she took another look around the room and found Teah sitting with Ace. Again, the dim-wit Teah still wouldn't look at her, but Ace did. He glared at her in an intimidating manner, then gave her the sign to back off. Ace was a scary guy, and Lindsey wanted no dealing with him, so she quickly looked way.

So far things were not working out for her today, so she would have to come up with another plan for Danny, and she would have to come up with another fall guy. Damn it, Teah! She should have known to have a plan B when dealing with Teah because everybody knows that she has broken toys in the attic.

The side doors of the church opened, and the family came in and sat in the first rows of benches near the casket. Lindsey quickly found Danny, she hadn't seen her in 4 years and secretly hoped that she had gotten fat with the heartbreak and leaving town, overeating would have been great. But sadly, Lindsey observed, Danny hadn't gained an ounce. She looked great as always but for right now, seeing the brokenhearted grief on her face gave Lindsey a little pleasure. It was like the pleasure she had gotten when Danny learned that she was pregnant with Kevin's baby, four years ago.

Thinking back to the day when she had destroyed, Danielle Elizabeth Johnston, put a vindictive smile on her face.

It was Derby day in Kentucky, and everyone in their crowd was at Anthony and Lauren's new home for one of Anthony's famous barbecues. Just thinking about all of the people who had attended the cookout almost made her wet her panties because they all witnessed Danny's fall from grace. Her parents, Deacon Paul Harris and Delores Harris, Sara Williams, Lauren and Kevin's mother were there, Teah's mom Amanda Howard and Ace's mother, Mary-Rose Malone were there, drunk but still useful spectators, and of course Chief Johnston and Miss Wilma. Other people attended the derby party, but the parents of her best friends were the main guests that needed to observe firsthand what was about to happen.

She could hardly wait for Danny and Kevin to get to the party because it would be their last date. At 3:05 that afternoon, they came around to the back of the Porter's house arm in arm as the D. J. played, "I'm Every Woman" by Chaka Khan. "How fitting, how right," she thought as she began to shake her leg.

After the song had finished playing, her dad, Deacon Paul Harris came to the porch of the shack, took the mic and called for everyone's attention. "Today I have a special announcement to make. I am so proud to announce our little girl Lindsey and Kevin Williams are engaged!" A hush came over the crowd, and everyone looked at Kevin and Danny with questions on their faces. To break the spell, the Deacon urged, "Let's give these young lovers a round of applause." The clapping was weak because all hell broke loose. Danny slapped Kevin hard in the face and ran from the party, Miss Wilma went after her. Then Chief Johnston grabbed Kevin's throat and started choking him. Anthony and Slicks pulled them apart. Lauren went after Lindsey, but her mother, Delores Harris, stepped in front of her daughter and hissed, "You better not touch her! She is pregnant and I will have you arrested."

Although, Lindsey thought with regrets, she did not go home with her baby's father and intended husband, it was a great night to remember. The next day Danny left Louisville, which was more icing on the cake. This meant she didn't have to worry about Kevin trying to get back with her. After that night, he would have a snow ball's chance in hell making up with that bitch, but the next step in her plan would have ended her for good. 'Damn you, Teah!' She thought.

The sun shone brightly through the colorful stained glass windows of the church, giving the church warmness in contrast to the sadness of the 12 o'clock funeral services. As the Soloist began to sing, "Nearer My God to Thee," Lauren took one last look around the church to see where her *friends* were sitting. Teah was seated on the far right of the church with Ace, and Lindsey sat in the middle pew beside an older couple. Looking at her former friend and sister-law, Lauren noticed that Lindsey seemed to be upset. Well, everyone loved Samantha Nicole Johnston, always smiling and enjoying her life. There was a great picture of her atop of the casket, with an enormous smile on her face, showing off her well-shaped and very white teeth. This made Lauren tear up.

It seemed like time was going far too fast for Danny. When Danny focused again, she was being led to a seat in the graveyard. Her mind kept flashing back through her life with her sister. How she had comforted Sam for her first day at grade school, how they both accepted Christ at the same time, protecting Sam from bullies, beating Sam mercifully at tennis, Sam's first prom, the fights they had about Slicks and the last time they exchanged "I love yous." Tears flowed down her face, she could hear her aunt and uncle's grief, but she couldn't look at them. There wasn't any room in her mind for anyone but Sam.

Then it happened, all of a sudden the Pastor was saying, "Ashes to ashes, dust to dust, from dust we came, and to dust we must return."

Standing Danny screamed, "No, this can't be over, SAMANTHA!"

She kneeled to the ground near where the casket was sitting and wept loudly. Everyone at the grave site began to wail at the sight of such grief. Chief J was trying to get to Danny, but Miss Wilma had lost all composure, so he signaled to Kevin to help.

As Kevin hurried toward the woman that he loved, the Harris' rushed from the graveyard because it was imperative for them not to witness firsthand how Kevin could insult his wife, their daughter, by choosing to comfort his ex-lover.

When Danny was on her knees crying painfully into her hands, the person was delighted.

"This bitch should cry! I want to see her begging me not to kill her, like her sister, "Please don't hurt me! Please don't hurt me!" I knew she would come home for her sister's funeral! Now I will get her! Danielle must die! She is a sinner! All sin must be wiped out! I will get her! I can't wait to put my blade into her and watch the sinful blood pour from her body. I can't let her live! She's not right! I want her to die! Die! Die!"

In the person's delight at the sight of Danny's misery, the words that were supposed to stay inside its head were now slipping out of its mouth in a loud whisper. Questionly, a nearby mourner looked at the person, so the person covered its face, and wept loudly. The mourner patted the person's shoulders.

As ministers, Nurses Guild, and some of the members of the Ladies Auxiliary Committee came forward and began to comfort the family, Lindsey Williams wiped her face and slipped quietly from the service. Although she had been crying for a very different reason, she had to make sure plan b was still coming along. 'This is the end for Ms. Johnston,' Lindsey thought as she crept away.

Using all of her strength, Lauren walked up to the front and said, "This concludes the services for Samantha Nicole Johnston. Ephesians Baptist Church Ladies Auxiliary has prepared dinner at the Johnston's home 932 South 47th Street. Please proceed there at this time, thank you for coming."

Lauren nodded for Anthony to start leading people away from the grave site to give the family some private time.

Kevin pulled Danny from the ground into his arms, where she went eagerly for warmth from the coldness she felt from the grave. By the time the limo carrying the Johnston's left the graveyard, Kevin had managed to get Danny to sit in one of the nearby chairs. Still holding him and sobbing she asked, "What am I going to do without Sam, Kevin?"

"What would Sam want you to do?"

"She would want me to live large and be happy, but I can't be happy without my sister."

"Danny, you have no choice. If you can't move on for your sake, do it for Sam. Do the things she would want to see you do. I believe she can rest in peace knowing that you are ok."

Wiping her face with one of the tissues, left by the Ladies Auxiliary Committee, she said sadly, "I wish I could see some sign that she was alright."

"Spoken like a true big sister…" He was interrupted by the chirping of a bright red Cardinal bird sitting on Sam's casket.

"Kevin, look!" she whispered. They looked at the bird unable to move until it flew away.

"What do you think? Was it a sign from her?"

"It can be whatever you think it is, remember you asked the question."

"Well, she's in a heavenly place, now. I will just have to get used to not having her here with me."

"I believe she is with you every day in spirit. You will hear her words when you need comfort, sometimes you will even talk to her out loud but above all don't fight grief because you think it's a sign of weakness. If you need to cry, cry. You will do a lot of that until you can laugh with her."

"Kevin Williams, how are you so sure of these actions?"

"Remember my Uncle Rick? He was my mentor when my father left us, and when he died, I suffered. I learned about grief the hard way. I had no one to help me. He was my mother's only brother, so no help there; he was my sister's hero, no help there."

They were quiet for a moment, then Danny asked, "What about us?"

"We will be together no matter what happens. You want to talk things out today or tomorrow?"

"Today is good." She said looking at the casket that held her sister. "Life is short and unsure one way or another, I must get on with my life, whatever that is."

Kissing her on the lips, he suggested, "Let's go before Chief Johnston chokes me again, just when I think he's warming up to me."

This made her laugh for the first time in a long time and she said, "Don't be so sure."

Danny stood, then reached down and touched the casket she said, "Goodbye, Sam. I love you, and I always will."

Holding hands as they walked through the graveyard to the Lincoln, two more Kentucky Cardinal Birds flew across their paths. For the first time in a long time, the couple felt that things would finally work out for them.

CHAPTER TWELVE

When they entered the home where she had grown up, she felt the warmness and safety that it had always offered. Everyone was there, but this time, instead of hiding from them, Danny accepted their condolences and heartfelt thoughts of good will. She patiently listened to stories from well-wishers about Sam and realized that her sister had touched many lives in her short 23 years.

"Hello," Dr. Clayton Parker said to Danny. "You must be Samantha's sister, I can see the similarities. I am Dr. Clayton Parker, and I worked with your sister at The East Madison Street Drug Rehabilitation Center."

"Oh!" Danny said, "How are you, Dr. Parker? I am so glad that you came out to show your support for Sam."

"Samantha was a great person. We are going to miss her very much. She cared about the patients and staff members. She was always looking out for others."

In a hushed voiced he said, "You know I was threatened by that man over there, he said his name was *Slicks*. The things he said he would do to me if I spoke to "Baby Cakes," --his words, again, made me puke when he left. I just wanted y'all to know that I didn't mean to hurt Samantha. It was just one of those days, and I took it out on her. I will regret that action forever. I just want you to know that I would never intentionally hurt anyone."

"I would have been her mentor if she had lived."

"That is nice to know, too. Thank you so much for coming here today." Danny said, trying to end the strange conversation.

"Sadly, I must leave this delightful celebration of life because I am on duty, and there is an awful lot of interest in our conversation."

Danny turned to look in the direction that Dr. Parker had been staring as he talked to her. She saw that Kevin, Unc, Anthony, and Slicks were looking at them intensely.

When she turned back to the doctor, he was already exiting out of the front door. There were crowds of people eating, talking, going and coming, but Danny was determined to greet them all. Well, well, her next greeters were Deacon and Mrs. Harris. Why on earth were they here? Danny questioned.

Stiffly, they granted their condolences for her sister's death. It was so awkward that she was grateful when Auntie Wilma called her to the phone.

As she left their presence, she could feel their relief as well as her own. Danny surmised that they had come because of their duties in the church. He was a Deacon and she was a member of the Ladies Auxiliary Committee so, they had to be civil and show support for the Johnston family in their time of grief.

On the other end of the call was Lauren.

"Where are you?" Danny asked.

"Just taking my baked chicken out of the oven to bring over there, but I've got something to show you. Can you come over here quickly? But don't bring your police friends."

"What is it?" Danny asked, whispering but she really didn't have to because the house was filled with visitors, and friends. The many conversations were loud and noisy.

"I've got some news about Sam's death, but we can't tell anyone until we get the whole story. Hurry and remember not to let anybody know."

The line went dead.

Danny surveyed the crowd of people to see who was looking, but no one was watching her at that moment, so she slipped out the side door leading to the patio. Walking down the driveway, she could see that Slicks 1994 navy blue Pontiac Grand Prix was the last one parked and to her surprise, the keys were in it. Turning off the radio before she started the car, she backed quietly out of the driveway.

She headed around the parkway as she had done so many times before. She noticed with pleasure how smoothly Slicks' car handled as she took the curves of Southwestern Parkway at speeds well over the speed limit. She laughed at the irony of being stopped by the police but that didn't happen. She parked the Grand Prix on the street, just to be cautious because she didn't know what was going on at the Porter's house. She'd left the keys in the car for a quick getaway in case there were any trouble. She trusted Lauren, but why didn't she call Anthony with this information? It wasn't like her to go alone on something as serious as Sam's murder.

She never knocked on their door, so she let herself into the house by the kitchen door.

"Hey, Lauren! What's up?" she called walking into the kitchen rich with the baked chicken aroma.

But nothing could prepare her for what she saw when she turned the corner of the spacious kitchen. Lauren was tied to a chair.

"What the hell...?" she started to say, but she was punched hard in the left side of her face.

The punch in the face knocked her to the floor. She was about to blackout, but she fought the feeling with all the strength she had in her body. She pulled herself up by holding onto the side of the kitchen island.

When her eyes cleared, she saw Lindsey and some strange man.

"See, I told you she was a hard nut to crack," Lindsey said with this sick tone in her voice.

"Lindsey, what is going on?" Danny managed to say firmly but she felt unsteady on her feet.

"This is my Uncle Don, You remember him, he's my dad's brother and a close friend of mine." Lindsey explained rubbing the dangerous looking man's chest.

The six foot three man was wearing a blue plaid shirt with the buttons open exposing his very hair chest. He had an arm around Lindsey's small waist and the other hand pointed a gun at Danny's heart.

Calmly, Danny asked, "Why is Lauren tied to the chair, Linds? What is going on?"

Leaving his embrace, Lindsey explained, "Well, Danny it is like this, I want you to leave my husband alone. And you just won't do that so I must teach you a lesson, bitch!"

Danny's heart was pounding in her chest, as she desperately tried to think of some way to appeal to her childhood friend. But looking at Lindsey now, Danny didn't know if she'd ever known her at all. She was dressed in a yellow halter top that looked like a Victoria Secrets lacy bra, and some Daisy Dukes denim shorts that were cut so high the checks of her butt was showing.

Stalling for time to think of a plan to save both her and Lauren, Danny decided to keep her talking. "What lesson is that?"

Leaning over the kitchen island so Uncle Don could see her behind with the denim strip in the middle, Lindsey replied, "You are going to watch Uncle Don rape Lauren."

Lauren stifled a cry and tried in vain to free herself from the restraints.

Joining in Uncle Don added, "Once you see what I am going to do to your friend here, you won't come back to Louisville again." With a wicked smile he said, "Her rape will be all your fault and my pleasure."

Rubbing Lindsey's exposed buttocks, he continued his terrifying speech. Looking Danny directly in the eyes he said, "You see I taught Linds everything about how to please a man and she wants to please Kevin."

Then Lindsey French kissed the man who kept the gun on Danny.

Danny couldn't believe what she was seeing. She always knew that Lindsey was sneaky loose with her sexuality, but this was sick.

Lindsey slapped Danny and said, "Don't you judge me, bitch. I've been fucking him since I was ten. And I like it. However, I also like fucking Kevin and I will continue to do so."

"Have you thought this through Lindsey? Lauren will tell her husband, the police."

"No she won't," Uncle Don said, "When I get through with her, she will be too scared to tell anyone, because I promise I will do the same thing to her again only worse."

Then he licked Lauren on the side of her face. Feeling his disgusting saliva on her face caused Lauren to cry out. This time Lindsey slapped Lauren, "Shut up, bitch and enjoy!"

Lauren started to helplessly cry, which made Danny more desperate for a plan.

Being rational, she realized that there wasn't any way she could get herself and Lauren out of this situation soon, so it would have to play out until she could find a way to turn this standoff around. Maybe it wouldn't be long before someone realized that she was gone so, she'd have to play along.

Danny knew that she must do something, or Lauren would be raped by this mad man. She didn't know if she should wait and let him start the sexual assault and then stop him or offer herself up to him now. "Yes," her mind thought. "Offering myself to Uncle Don may cause Lindsey to become jealous. She is envious of me and Kevin, so just maybe she will feel the same way about seeing me with her sick Uncle Don."

"Wait!" Danny countered, "Why not have sex with me first? Then Lindsey and I can compare notes on your performance?"

"What?!" Lindsey shouted to the deranged man, who had stopped looking at Lauren and was now focused on Danny. "No, Uncle Don! Fuck Lauren the same way you used to do me before I liked it, hard and fast."

Then he looked at Lauren again with new lust in his eyes. Danny's mind screamed, "Think like a whore!"

Danny hopped on the kitchen island, spread her legs and said, "Bring it to me, lover boy. If you like, I will fight you like I don't want it, but I do want it, feel me? If it's good enough for Lindsey, then I know I can make you feel better.

I've always done things better than her. Come on, try me," she teased pulling up her dress to show a pair of tiny, red-striped panties.

This was too much for the mad man, handing the gun to Lindsey, he started toward Danny.

"No, Uncle Don, she can't have you. You are all mine."

He stopped long enough to push Lindsey to the floor. "Get out of my way, bitch!"

Lauren was screaming, "No, Danny!"

Uncle Don slapped Lauren without even looking at her and continued across the room to the island where Danny lay half-dressed and waiting for him but that was the last step he ever took.

Meanwhile at the Johnston's house, Slicks and Ace came into the Chief's den looking for Kevin and Anthony.

"Ace gave me some information that you should hear."

Getting up from the couch with a bourbon in his hand, the Chief said, "What's up, Ace?"

"You see, Teah and me, we've got this thing going on between us. Well, at the funeral she came to me and told me that Lindsey was bullying her because she wanted her to do something that she didn't want to do. The service was just starting, so I gave Lindsey the warning sign, and I thought no more about it until we got here at the house. Teah couldn't be still and she was very upset, so I made her tell me. She said that she was supposed to get Danny alone in the Shack, and she and Lindsey were going to get rid of her."

"The Shack?" Anthony questioned. "How was she going to do that?"

"Teah told me that she was supposed to call Danny with information about Sam…"

"Where is Danny?" Kevin asked.

"Where is my wife?" Anthony asked.

They ran from the house while calling for back up. When they got to the driveway, Slicks realized that his car was gone.

They all thought, "Danny."

The Lincoln was parked on the street, so they all piled in it as Kevin put on the police flasher and floored the big car around the parkway towards Anthony's house.

They turned off the sirens as they approached the house. The men looked like they were playing out a scene from a classic movie. With guns drawn, they hunched down and crept toward the shack. They heard a loud booming gunshot and then screams coming from the kitchen.

When Danny saw Lindsey turn the gun from Lauren to her perverted Uncle Don, she rolled off the island and pulled Lauren to the floor, chair and all. This would be her chance to save them she thought, but all of sudden there were footsteps and shouting coming from above them.

Anthony had knocked Lindsey to the floor, taking the gun from her and giving it to Ace.

Slicks came around the island and helped Danny up, while Uncle J untied Lauren.

"Call an ambulance and the medical examiner," Anthony told Ace while he handcuffed Lindsey.

"Is he dead?" Lindsey asked and just for a moment, Kevin thought he saw a smile creep across his wife's face.

"Kevin, this is a mistake. Uncle Don tried to rape us. I had to shoot him." Lindsey explained.

"Cut the crap, Lindsey!" Kevin hissed. "We know the whole story."

Gazing up from the floor and looking very innocent, Lindsey continued to explain. "No, you don't. He's been raping me since I was ten, Kevin. He made me bring him here so he could rape all of us."

As Anthony read her the Miranda rights, she started screaming, "No! This can't happen. I am a good Christian girl. Kevin, help me!"

Anthony and Kevin stood her up and she whirled to face Danny. Lindsey screeched in a high pitched voice, "I hate you, bitch! You still didn't win. I made sure I got pregnant again, and I made sure it was Kevin's. You will never be rid of me!" She then lowered her voice so low that it made her almost sound like a demon. She continued, "This ain't over, bitch. You will be dead by tomorrow! Kevin, you ain't nothing but a dog."

"You're right Linds, an untied dog!" then he looked at Anthony and said, "Get her out of my sight!"

More officers entered the kitchen as Lindsey was being lead out by Anthony. The paramedics had also arrived to examine Lauren and Danny, but when they looked for Danny, she was nowhere to be found. Kevin's heart was in his throat as he and Uncle J ran to the street just in time to see the Lincoln turn right onto the parkway.

Chief J turned to Kevin and said very seriously, "You need to go after her. She has had too much today. Now is the time to straighten out what is wrong between the two of you.

I will stay here and do what I can to help Anthony and the boys, but Danny needs you more."

The Chief just marveled at Slicks timing, that boy seems to always be at the right place at the right time, he thought watching Kevin and Slicks run toward the Pontiac. He probably feels like he is saving Samantha over and over again, the older man concluded as he walked back to the house to help out where ever he was needed.

CHAPTER THIRTEEN

Kevin was so stunned by what had just taken place that he could only drive in silence. Although this was Slicks' car, it was silently understood that he would drive. Slick knew that Kevin could not just sit in the passenger seat while his mind drove him crazy. The only mental therapy at this point was to split the trauma of Kevin's life spinning out of control with the concentration needed to drive safely. Slicks only wished that he had a second chance to go to the woman that he would love forever. Looking at Kevin he thought, don't blow it this time.

So much had happened today that Kevin didn't even know where to begin to think, but the solution came to him quickly as he remembered the Chief's advice. When he caught up with Danny, they would solve their problem once and for all. She was going to listen to him even if he had to tie her down. Danny was scared, traumatized, and alone, just maybe her defenses were down far enough for her to accept what he had to say. He knew it was wishful thinking, but after today anything was possible.

Danny had parked the Lincoln on the shoulder of a park along River Road, and she was just standing there looking at the mighty Ohio River. This is what she always did when there was a crisis in her life. He should have known that this was where she was headed. She never turned her head as he pulled the Grand Prix beside the Lincoln.

As Slicks entered the driver side of his car, Kevin said, "Thanks, man."

Slicks just nodded as he eased the Pontiac onto River Road.

Storm clouds were rolling in over the Ohio River causing the waves to slap noisily against its banks but Kevin realized that the emotional storm was about to begin in his personal life as Danny walked toward him. Her face was twisted with rage and anger.

All of a sudden his head snapped back, and he felt a sharp, stinging pain radiating across his face.

Danny had slapped him hard, and she was prepared to do it again. He had to grab both of her hands to keep her from continuing the assault on his body.

Screaming she said, "This is all your fault, damn you!"

He knew that she could do more harm to him because the Chief had taught her and her sister how to defend themselves. Thinking of what had happened to Ace, he knew that he had to get her out of this murderous mode.

"Stop it, Danny!" He said in a commanding voice, hoping to cause her to pause in her struggle against him but she was violently angry, she tried to head-butt him, but he dodged that move, and she got out of his grip.

Now facing him, she shrieked, "Because of you, your sister and I were nearly raped, your wife tried to kill me, and my sister is dead!" she continued her attack on him.

He'd vowed long ago to never to lay hands on a woman because his father had been an abuser, but he had to think of something to get her under control. So the next time she swung at him, he caught both of her balled fists, and turned her body so that her back was up against his body. Using his knees, he pushed the back of her knees causing her to slide with him to the ground. He held her there until the screaming and struggling stopped.

Sitting there with a full body hold on Danny, the rain began to fall on them, and soon they were soaking wet from the beginning of the spring rains but he knew that he couldn't just let her out of the hold until she was entirely rational again.

"Ok, Kevin let me go," Danny asked calmly.

"Is this over?" He asked softly in her ear.

"Oh, it is so over." She sniffed, and he could feel her body no longer resisting his hold.

"Oh, it's over" was a play on words, he thought while loosening his grip on her body but not her hands.

Taking the hint that she may be talking about how it was over between the two of them he said, "This may be over for you, but you promised to discuss our problems through."

Danny didn't answer.

It had been a long and difficult day for both of them and the strain of the day was getting to them. Now Kevin was feeling angry, and he hissed in her ear.

"We are going to talk if it kills us. Now I am going to let you go, and you are going to get in the car, or I will stuff you in there!"

Releasing her, he watched as she walked to the Lincoln and got in on the passenger side and slammed the door. Only then did he breathe a sigh of relief, but he knew that the feeling would not last for a long. Looking at her face through the car's window he thought, "She's the definition of an angry black woman." But this next round he would have to win because he needed his life back. His life had been in limbo for 4 years and as he started the car he figured that now was the time to take it back with or without Danny. No matter how badly it would hurt to go on without her, he needed to move on.

The storm's intensity increased as Kevin maneuvered the Lincoln down River Road. The lightning flashed vividly, the thunder was violently rolling, shaking the land, and the rainfall was nearly blinding, but he drove on. The weather seemed to mirror their shattered lives.

Soon he pulled into a worn gravel driveway that wound through a wilderness of wild trees and tall grass. After the car's motor had been turned off, he sprinted to the door of a rustic cabin.

Danny examined the cabin and wondered who lived in this place that looked like the cabin in the Beverly Hillbillies sitcom. The one story small dwelling was the classic wood and white mortar. Looking at this structure would bring pioneer days to mind. It was nestled in the center of trees that nearly surrounded the cabin. As she exited the car, she noticed that she could hear the Ohio River slamming against its banks. The weather seemed to reflect her mood at this time, very turbulent.

She ran from the car through the pouring rain to the open cabin door where she found Kevin on his knees building a fire in the ash-laden fireplace.

Without looking or turning from his task, Kevin said, "The bathroom is down the hall. Go take a shower. I will bring you some dry clothes."

Slowly, she went through the house noticing that the inside of the place looked better than the outside, but still the question remained, who lives here?

Only after the warm water started gently pelting her body did she start to relax from the life changing events of the day. Burying her sister, nearly being raped, killed, being betrayed, not once but twice, by a childhood friend, and now the confrontation that was about to happen with Kevin. Looking up as if looking to the heavens, she thought, "Can this day get any worse?"

She must have been in deep thought because she didn't hear Kevin leaving towels and clothes on the sink for her. Taking a large brown washcloth from the stack, she continued with her shower.

While drying off, she looked around the tiny bathroom; she noticed that there were no signs of female life. The bathroom was the center of a woman's world. The walls were bare of decorations, and the shower curtain was a nondescript tan. She decided to look in the medicine cabinet, only to find a shaving razor, face cream for men, toothpaste and mouthwash. Nothing said that a woman had ever been here. Perhaps, she concluded, it was a rental but in her opinion, it could look more cheery.

She wondered what type of clothes he had that would fit her. Unfolding the sweat pants and sweatshirt that had LPD written across them, she realized the answer to that question. He didn't, the sweats were his.

Putting on the large footies she padded her way back to the living room.

Kevin was sitting there gazing at the fire, but he turned when she entered the room.

"Do you still love me, Danny?"

The question gave her a jolt that made her physically jerk.

"What a question, Kevin after four years?"

"Cut the crap, Danny and answer the question. Do you still love me?"

She paused for a moment while he watched her intensively.

Hearing her Uncle's voice in her head, she lowered her defense and said, "Yes, I do."

"Then you have to listen to what I'm going to say. It's going to hurt but come hell or high water, I need my life back and I know you need some closure to this situation, too."

Nodding in agreement, she sat down in a chair near the fire.

"Let's start from the beginning, when I took Lindsey to the dance she seduced me."

"What?!" Danny exclaimed. "Really Kevin, that's your excuse for ruining our lives?!"

"Look!" He shouted, "She was your friend! Did you ever picture yourself being almost raped by her manipulations?"

"No, but I blame you for sleeping with her."

"So do I, but it did happen, and I can't take it back."

"Oh, don't leave out the part where she got pregnant and please don't leave out how you did the honorable thing and married her." Now she was standing in front of the large picture window. "Oh! And now I hear she is pregnant again! Did she seduce you again? Kevin, where is the good part of this story for me?"

"Sit down, Danny and listen. You promised."

Sitting back down she said, "I wish I hadn't made that promise."

"But you did, and I am holding you to it. Danny, Lindsey only has my name. We are married in name only. I don't live with her, I live here. Her family asked me to keep this quiet until after the baby was born but she lost the baby and they begged me to keep our living arrangements quiet until Lindsey could recover from losing our child.

The surprise of his words felt like the cold downpour of rain that she had just run through.

"What?!"

"We were in the middle of an annulment when Sam was killed."

"Oh, Kevin! Do you think she killed Sam? Lindsey and the Zombie that attacked me both said the same words, "This ain't over, bitch." Becoming concerned for her safety, she asked, "Is she the Zombie? Is she locked up?"

"I don't know what to think. I am afraid to say that she is the one. What if I'm wrong? I am sure Lindsey's in jail and after what she pulled today, she won't get out on bail. You are safe with me right now." Kevin assured Danny. "And I do know that right now, at this moment, we have got to put our lives back into some kind of perspective. I can't live like this anymore. With or without you I've got to move on. What's it going to be?"

"How, Kevin? So much has happened to us. In fact, she said that she was pregnant again with your child. How much do you expect from me? I love you, but I can't accept that she is having your baby. I don't want to be connected with her ever again."

"If Lindsey is pregnant, I am sure that the baby is not mine. I only slept with her one time, and that was the time that ruined my life."

"So, Kevin you never lived with her as her husband?"

"No, I couldn't."

After a moment of processing, she said, 'Are you involved with someone now?"

"I date every now and then but nothing serious. How about you? I know that something was going on between you and some professor."

"You were spying on me?"

"I guess you thought that I could let you walk out of my life and not know where you were or who you were with. Did you forget what I do for a living?"

For the first time in a long time, she smiled.

"Nothing serious, he wanted more, but I didn't have it to give."

"I want more, Danny. Can we try again?"

"There is a big mountain ahead of us, Kevin. When the news breaks about your wife, the sexual assault, and the man she killed, how can we present ourselves as a couple to our families, the church, and the community?"

Comforted that she was considering the idea of getting back together, he took a scene from Miss Wilma's playbook and said, "Miss Wilma would say that in difficult times like this, 'If God is for us then who can be against us?' or who can stop us?"

She smiled, reflecting on the woman who had lovingly raised her and her sister, " Miss Wilma would say, "Danny, don't throw the baby out with the dirty bathwater."

"Our water is filthy, so you have to be committed to our relationship. Danny, it's not going to be easy, but just don't run away from me again, please."

Standing, he pulled her into his arms, and again he asked, "Please."

Hearing his heart pounding inside his body she knew that he was begging for this partnership to start again and she wanted it to begin, but she was scared.

"I want us to be together, Kevin but I am afraid of being hurt again."

"I will never hurt you again. There has never been anyone that mattered to me in my life more than you."

"I am still afraid, but even so, I am willing to try this again."

Hearing the words that he had waited for four years to hear, caused his heart to soar higher than the storm clouds that were raging outside of the little cabin.

He kissed her, and that was the beginning of a well overdue night of passionate lovemaking, and love promising.

CHAPTER FOURTEEN

In the middle of night, groggy from love making and love planning, Danny heard Kevin calling the Johnstons to let them know that she was with him and that all was well. From what she heard of the one-sided conversation they were pleased, so it was easy for her to roll over and go back to sleep. When Kevin rejoined her in bed, she crawled over to him and drifted into a peaceful sleep.

Placing his arm around her, he wept silently while thanking the Lord for giving back to him the love of his life.

At 1 o'clock that morning the phone rang, and Kevin sleepily answered. Danny heard him say some words and hang up so, she drifted back to sleep.

Moments later he woke her, "I've got to go into town to see some man about his daughter. The gun is under my pillow."

Frowning up at him, she asked, "What's wrong, Kevin?"

"Nothing that I know of, but there is some strange man refusing treatment at the hospital until he tells me about his daughter."

"Work. I get that but why the gun? Does this have anything to do with our case?"

"I don't think so. Remember, I have been removed from our case. The gun is for your protection. Did you see where this cabin is located? I don't want to leave you without protection. I doubt that you will need it, but it's there if you do." Kissing her he said, "I'll be back as soon as I can."

She went to the window and watched him pull off into the pouring down rain. He was right, the cabin was so secluded and eerie. Turning away from the window, she went back to the bedroom and back to sleep. But sometime later, thoughts started coming to her mind about her and Kevin. It seemed so strange not to hate him and Lindsey. There was an empty hole in her soul where scorn and loathing had lived for four years. She didn't know how to begin to live with all that had happened in a few short days.

Outside the storm continue to rage, lightning flashes were increasing making the dark bedroom seem like daytime. Danny snuggled deeper into the covers and listened to the rain pounding on the roof of the cabin. The rhythm of the down pour seemed to make her feel relaxed, so she drifted off to sleep again.

Her sleep kept being interrupted by the wind beating up against the sides of the cabin. Sitting up, Danny listened carefully to the noise to determine if what she heard was storm noises or something else.

"She was with me. Didn't Miss Wilma tell you that I called to let you know that Danny was safe with me?"

"No! She just poisoned me. Go get Danny. Kevin, she is going to kill her!" The visibly shaken man cried.

"I'm going."

At the nurse's station, he didn't ask to use the phone, he just went behind the counter and picked up the receiver of the phone. After punching in some numbers, he shouted, "This is Lieutenant Kevin Williams. I need officers. Send the police to 4492 Elrio Road! Attempted Murder is in progress!"

Kevin turned and ran out of the hospital to his car. It was a long ride to the cabin, but he would go with lights blazing at high speed. He sent a prayer up to God, "Please don't let me lose the woman that I love." He couldn't even begin to focus on what the Chief had said. He just needed to get to Danny before it was too late.

At the cabin the weather outside had not let up, it was still thundering and lightning, setting a grim scene for what was happening on the inside.

The vivid flash of lightning lit the kitchen to show Miss Wilma wearing the hideous and bizarre costume.

"Miss Wilma?" Danny whispered to the woman who had nourished her and her sister all of their lives. "What the hell?"

"Hell, it is for you." The woman smiled with a fiendish look on her face.

Keeping her finger on the trigger and the gun pointed at center mass, Danny continued to be shocked.

"You killed Sam."

"No, baby, I killed sin." With her voice rising, while swinging the knife the mad woman explained. "You see my life has been a big fat lie. Thanks to your father. I have to correct all of that and make it right."

"My father's dead. What are you talking about?"

"Your father will be dead in a few minutes. You see, I killed him too." Then she laughed, making a sound that came straight from the pits of hell.

"What are you talking about?" Danny wanted answers from the woman she'd always gone to for comfort. She wanted answers from the woman who she may have to kill in order to save herself. Danny couldn't pay any attention to the blood flowing down the front of the t-shirt. She had to focus on what was in front of her.

"J is your father, yours and Sam's." She almost sang the phrase as if it were a song. Thunder boomed again causing Danny to jump, but she held the gun on the deranged woman holding the knife.

"They thought I didn't know, but I did. J loved your mother. He never loved me. Your uncle who you thought was your daddy married her because he was gay and wanted to cover his career with a family. When he got killed in the war, I killed your mother, because you understand, J would have eventually left me for her and I couldn't live through that so she had to go. I raised both you and your sister as if you were my children. Then Sam told me the other day that she was doing a family tree with DNA and blood and such. I knew the truth would come out so, she had to go too. Now it is your turn to join your other family members in hell."

Danny dropped to the floor and pulled the throw rug that went from one side of the table to under Miss Wilma. This caused the older woman to fall backward and hit her head on the corner of the counter. Picking up the gun, Danny ran to the fallen killer and kicked her in the head, to make sure she wasn't faking being knocked out by the fall.

Danny sprinted to the living room and looked at the door for a fast exit from hell. With her heart beating wildly in her chest she knew that both locks on the door couldn't be opened quickly. Thankfully, she found a thick log and threw it at the picture window causing it to explode. As she jumped out of the window, pieces of glass sliced into her feet, and she paused just long enough to pull out the pieces that would prevent her from running, the rest of the glass would have to stay until later. She moved to the shelter of a large tree, and then looked back at the house. No one was coming after her.

Somewhere in her conscious mind, she wanted to cry, but if she wanted to survive this attack she'd better concentrate on living. The rain was pouring down on her as she entered the deepest part of the wilderness. At the rate the blood was coming from her shoulder, Danny knew it wouldn't be long before she would pass out. Barefoot and bleeding from the shoulder and feet, she leaned against the tree for support. She needed to think, should she hide or fight? She just couldn't see herself fighting a woman who'd loved and cared for her most of her life. Just then a hand went around her mouth, and she shot the person in the upper arm.

He screamed, "Damn, Danny!"

"Slicks?!" she replied almost begging because after the week she had she didn't know who could be showing up to kill her.

"Dan, you shot me!"

"I thought you were trying to kill me, too."

"No, I came to save you." He said wrapping his belt around his arm.

"Ace told me where you were, so I came to be sure you were ok. That's when I saw Miss Wilma putting on this strange 'Night of the living dead' garb and go through the back door."

Looking at her he said, "You're bleeding. Here use my shirt to apply pressure." Taking off his shirt and handing it to her, he continued. "Danny, stay here, get in these bushes and keep the pressure on your shoulder. I am going for help.'

"Slicks, be careful. Please! I don't know what is wrong with Miss Wilma, but she is dangerous."

He just said, "Sit tight. Keep the gun in your hand and for gosh sake, don't shoot me again."

He took off toward the cabin. Danny started to pray. Pray, Danny thought, who taught me to pray? Miss Wilma. Who's trying to kill me? Miss Wilma. At that moment she realized, whatever happened, her faith would not be doubted. Not now so, she continued to pray for herself, Slicks, and her newly found father.

Kevin had the Lincoln traveling at high speed toward the cabin off of River Road. He was hoping that the road wouldn't flood as it usually did from time to time during a heavy downfall of rain. Somewhere in the distance, the sirens' of many police cars were blaring. They were headed to his cabin but they were too far away to give him any comfort so he began to pray for Danny's safety. He looked in the glove compartment of the Lincoln for his backup gun and put it on the seat. He thought of how strange it was going to be to hopefully arrest and not kill the woman he'd respected all of his life. The only thing he could conclude about the whole situation was that he and Danny were in the middle of a double triangle. Mind blowing, but he drove on through the night not knowing what he would find when he got to the cabin.

CHAPTER FIFTEEN

Danny huddled down in the bushes trying to evaluate her ticking-bomb situation and plan her next steps. Miss Wilma had taught them to always have a plan b. What? Miss Wilma's words again! Her mind screamed. The giant ball of emotions that she had squashed down earlier started to rise in her throat, and she began to cry. No! She stopped herself. "Don't give in. If you cry, you die," her brain shouted. The Lord above knew how much she loved Miss Wilma, but she could not let the woman kill her. She could hear Miss Wilma's voice in her head again," Danielle Elizabeth Johnston! I've raised strong children! My kids fight back when life is trying to bring them down! They are strong in their faith! Are you still walking with God, Danny?! Don't hesitate, are you?!"

That was her wake up call. The person who was trying to kill her was not the person who had raised her. It was unbearable to think that she would rely on the strength of the individual who had loved her and taught her how to be strong just so she could take down that same person who now wanted her dead but so be it, she decided. Although she was scared out of her mind, she would fight back with all of the courage Miss Wilma had instilled in her. This was insane, but she realized that this wasn't the time to examine the very strange situation. Her only goal now was to survive.

A loud clap of thunder rolled across the dark skies at the same time that a boom of gunfire spliced through the storm. After the boom, she heard a male let out a piercing and agonizing scream. Her heart slammed hard in her chest as she realized that Slicks was down and not coming back for her.

Now was the time for plan B. "I can't sit here and let her find me." She thought. Looking at her shoulder where the mad Miss Wilma had stabbed her, she assessed that the bleeding had slowed down thanks to Slicks. Her feet were just leaking a little blood from the broken glass she'd walked through after she had broken the picture window, but some small pieces were still in her feet.

After the assessment, Danny decided that now was the time to take the fight to Miss Wilma. She had to focus on the fact that the woman she was hunting was not the woman who had lovingly raised her and her sister Sam, but a woman who wanted her dead.

Lightning flashed as she stood from her hiding place, making her feel like she was in a scene from Friday the 13th

or Halloween, where the lone survivor takes a stand against the knife-wielding villain.

Slicks' scream seemed to have come from the west side of the cabin. There was plenty of foliage to give her cover. Creeping through the woods during a storm near the cabin was eerie but so was jumping at any sound that wasn't made by the rain.

Just as she got to the cabin, she saw Miss Wilma coming around the side of the cabin still carrying the large knife that was dripping with blood.

"Slicks," her mind called as her heart sank. She knew that she had to move fast if there was a chance to save Slicks. Stepping out from the wilderness she could hear the sirens in the distance, but sadly they would be too late to help her and Slicks. She was feeling dizzy now from the loss of blood, but she willed herself to confront the woman who was trying to murder her.

The murderous woman was scurrying toward the back of the cabin. Danny knew she couldn't let her get to the woods, so she called to her, "Wilma!"

The calling of her name seemed to startle her because everyone called her Miss Wilma and the voice that said it sounded like Danny's.

Turning to face Danny, Miss Wilma displayed a hellish smile on her face as she replied in a strange voice, "Danielle, you know not to call me Wilma. I'm Auntie Wilma or Miss Wilma. Now try that again, Missy."

"Focus on the target, Danny don't listen to the nonsense or taunting. Keep your goals in your forefront." This was a different voice in her head. It was her uncle's, or at this time and place, father's voice.

Danny didn't reply but kept the gun trained on the woman's head.

"I saved you for last because I knew that I would have trouble killing you. I knew that I could get my full revenge with you. You know they all did me wrong; your bitch mother, your closeted gay uncle, and that son-of-bitch father. I raised his bastard children!" Then she started laughing in the most horrific voice that Danny had ever heard.

Raising the knife, she cried, "Killing you will end my quest of ridding the world of Jay's mistakes. I will cut out his sin!"

Quicker than Danny could react, the deranged woman threw the knife which struck Danny in the same injured shoulder.

The initial pain from the knife sticking out of her shoulder caused her to scream, but the sight of the insane woman running toward her caused Danny to refocus and fire a shot from the gun, before falling to the wet mud slick ground.

Miss Wilma fell down too, but jumped back up like a demon from hell and continued to come after Danny.

Pulling the knife out of her shoulder caused the bleeding to increase, but still she struggled to stand. Then she fired a procession of bullets into the approaching woman. Knowing from past experience that she was probably wearing a protective vest, Danny aimed at the upper part of her body, headshots were included. Strangely, the bullets hitting Miss Wilma's body caused her to do a short dance before falling with a splash into a nearby puddle of muddy water.

Although Danny had emptied the gun into the now, not moving woman, she couldn't be sure that the demonic woman wouldn't just get up and keep trying to kill her so, she kept the gun trained on her while blood was steadily seeping out of her own body.

Danny could hear voices telling her to lower her weapon, but she couldn't lower it. What if Miss Wilma got up? No, she needed to keep it pointed at her just in case.

The sight of seeing multiple police strobe lights flashing as he neared the cabin, caused his heart to siege in his chest. Kevin slid the Lincoln next to a patrol car with both of its doors open. Exiting his vehicle he could hear shouts coming from the side of his cabin for someone to drop their weapon. He ran to the back with his badge in his hand, where he saw Danny standing over a downed Miss Wilma, with the gun still pointed at the woman's bleeding head.

Slowly walking toward her, Kevin spoke softly, "Danny, she's not a threat anymore, put the gun down."

Danny didn't respond. She kept her focus on the body on the ground, waiting for it to get up again, not realizing that her gun was empty.

Kevin walked to the side of Danny and using a little force took the gun from her hand. As soon as he did, she collapsed in his arms.

"Danny!" he called in a deep panic but when he looked at her, her eyes rolled back in her head and closed.

Anthony and Chief Taylor ran through the tall weeds near the back of the cabin while hearing the scream of a wounded animal. Both men pulled their guns and slowly approached the side of the cabin. When they reached the edge of the cabin, they saw six police officers with their weapons drawn, pointing at Kevin holding Danny's listless body. Chief Taylor ordered the men to stand down. The sight of him holding the woman that he loved caused them to stop in their tracks. It was like if they moved, then what they were seeing would be true.

The men stood there staring at the rain beating down on Kevin and Danny until a paramedic approached them.

"Sir, she's not dead, but he won't let us touch her. If we don't get her soon then she will be."

The words seemed to mobilize them, and slap them out of their state of denial.

Anthony went to a grieving Kevin, who was sitting in the mud rocking Danny back and forth and mournfully crying.

"She's not gone, man. She needs help, Kevin. Let the doctors help her."

Kevin didn't respond.

Anthony looked at Chief Taylor and shook his head, "I can't get through to him."

Chief Taylor said to the paramedics, "As soon as we take him down you take her." Then he nodded at Anthony.

The Chief took Kevin's left arm, at the same time Anthony took the right arm, and together they pinned a howling Kevin to the ground.

"Now!" Anthony shouted at the paramedics.

Quickly, the two paramedics took Danny's unconscious body from Kevin's grip and rushed her to the waiting ambulance. When they released the grip they had on him, he just laid on the wet ground and continued to moan like a wounded animal.

As Anthony and Chief Taylor watched the EMTs load Slicks into a second ambulance, a patrolman reported that Slicks had been shot and stabbed.

"Sir, it doesn't look good for either of them." The officer stated with sympathy. "But the older woman is dead. We are waiting for the medical examiner."

Anthony couldn't say a word; he was just in shock and couldn't seem to process any of what was happening in front of his eyes.

After about five minutes, Chief Taylor kneeled on the ground beside Kevin and shouted, "Ok, time to man up, Kevin! She's not dead, and she needs you! Get yourself together and help her live!"

Kevin sat up and looked at his boss and best friend.

"Look over there, Kevin! They are still working on her! If she were dead, they would have stopped! Now get over there and show her love and strength! She has managed to stay alive so far, but she needs you, now." Chief Taylor scolded.

Standing up Kevin wiped his face, and started toward to the ambulance where medical techs were still working on Danny.

Chief Taylor watched as the ambulance with Slicks took off towards the hospital. Then he said, "I thought this was over when we arrested the wife. I never would have imagined that this was a double triangle."

"I didn't see the killer being Miss Wilma. How does one recover from this?" Anthony asked.

Anthony was relieved when the Chief suggested that they go to the hospital to get some answers to their burning questions.

CHAPTER SIXTEEN

At the University of Louisville Hospital, former Chief Johnston was almost out of his mind with worry about what his wife was doing to his daughter. The doctors had pumped his stomach and given him something for his high anxiety, but he couldn't rest until he knew that Danny was alright. It was very hard for him to pray since all of this was his fault.

His secret life had cost him, the woman he loved, Gail-Ann, his baby daughter, Samantha, and maybe his wife and oldest daughter. He tried to suppress the painful memories of how he had destroyed not only his life but the lives of others but the memories came flooding back to his mind. He had been dating Wilma in the spring of that year just to have something to do. She was a good girl from a good home. Her father was the associate pastor of Ephesians Baptist Church, and her mother was the Adult Sunday school teacher. Everyone thought that they made a good couple but him. He just wanted to have good companionship with some sex to help conqueror his restlessness.

Then it happened, just like it had for Kevin- Wilma told him she was pregnant. Of course, he would have to marry her because there was an image to uphold; His image as a rising star in the police department and her image as the good

Christian girl. Now everyone was happy but him, but he never let it show.

Things were going along nicely, but Wilma lost the baby and went into a deep depression. The doctors thought that her mental condition would improve with time, but it got increasingly worse when her gynecologist confirmed the fact that she would never be able to have any more children. Jacob thought that Wilma may be suicidal, so he sought help for her by making an appointment with psychiatrist Gail-Ann Perkins, MD. As soon as he saw her sparks started to fly between them, so he willed himself to concentrate on Wilma's condition and to play down his feeling of freedom from the marriage by this loss.

The therapy started working for Wilma and the affair between Jacob, and Dr. Gail-Ann Perkins was working well, too. Looking back and trying to justify his actions, he remembered planning to divorce Wilma and marry the love of his life, but then her father, the assistant pastor of the church died. Could he leave his wife after she had suffered two deaths in a matter of 6 months? He couldn't bear the thought of being classified in the community as a "nasty dog," and he had his career to think about. Rising in the ranks of the police department required a stable home life among other things, but being married to Wilma and her tragedies made him look so responsible and reliable. He longed for much more. He wanted the love and the hot passion of Dr. Gail-Ann Perkins.

The second job he created served two purposes, to get away from his grieving wife and to spend time with Gail-Ann. This worked well until Gail-Ann announced to him that she was pregnant with his child, and she wasn't going to have an abortion.

Jacob Johnston rolled over in the hospital bed as if to get away from memories of the past, but they kept right on coming...

One day while he was in his office pondering his plight he got a visit from his older brother.

Edward explained to his brother that he would be applying for new stats in the army as captain, but there would be an inquiry because there were rumors about him being gay.

Looking at his brother, Jacob thought, "rumors?" Both family and friends had wondered if the older brother was gay. Jacob couldn't begin to count the number of fights he'd been in because someone had called his brother gay.

"What can I do?" his brother asked, "I can do my job better than anyone that applied, and I can't have the gay rumor holding me back. I don't want this to hold me back."

Then the great idea hit him. Edward needed to prove that he wasn't gay, and Gail-Ann needed a father, preferably one with the last name of Johnston, for their first baby, all he needed to do was convince them that this was a workable plan. At that time, both Gail-Ann and Edward thought it was a great idea, and it worked out well. Edward was promoted, and he and Gail-Ann continued to see each other. When Samantha, their second child, was born, he nearly asked Wilma for a divorce but seeing her sister-in-law pregnant again pushed her into another depression. Gail-Ann suggested a different doctor help Wilma because the situation was getting strange for her, too. First of all, she told him, if anybody found out that she was having an affair with a patient's husband, her career would be over. But her biggest problem with being Wilma's doctor was hearing her pour her heart out about a marriage that was never going to work. Gail-Ann tearfully told him how guilty she felt every time Wilma talked about holding on to the man they both loved. It got even creepier, Gail-Ann said, when Wilma asked for advice on how to spice up the marriage.

They selected a new doctor for Wilma, and they continued to see each other. Just being together when it was convenient wasn't enough. They wanted to be together openly as a couple, or even better, as man and wife. Just the thought of being together on holidays and waking up together was what they both longed for, but there was the long-suffering Wilma. Seeing that having an affair wasn't enough he and Gail-Ann started to make plans to be together. They knew that it would be hard at first, but together they could face the hell that would come from confirming their love.

There would be hell, but it wouldn't be from them announcing to the world that they were a couple; it would be from the pain of losing the woman that he loved. Gail-Ann died in a freak accident but the truth corrected him, Gail-Ann was murdered by his wife. The pain was great when he learned that she had passed away in a freak accident. He didn't think that he could go on living, but he couldn't give in to that pain because of the girls, Danny and Samantha. They were young and alone, so he had to make his home their home, and he had to comfort them and help them to accept that their mother was gone. So, tonight when Wilma told him that she had killed Gail-Ann, he thought that the overwhelming pain of that knowledge would kill him before the poison she'd given him. What had he done? Then tears cascaded down his face and rolled off into the pillow.

Just at that moment, there was a knock on the door, and the pastor of Ephesians Baptist Church came into the room to find Jacob Johnston bawling like a person who had lost all hope. The larger than life pastor went to the bed and hugged the Chief until he was spent of emotion.

"What can I do?" the pastor asked.

"I don't know what my needs are right now. I've messed up so many lives."

"Yet you must go on." The big man said, "You must be even stronger now, Jacob. I have news some of it is good, and some of it is bad."

With fresh tears swelled in his eyes, Jacob braced himself for the worst and said, "Let me have it."

"Well, Danny is in critical condition in ICU, Sylvester is in surgery, and your wife is dead."

To hear that Wilma was dead caused Jacob to break down again because he felt that he had been the cause of all of her troubles.

The patient pastor held Jacob's big hands in his until the wave of grief and regret passed.

In a weak, and whiney voice Jacob asked, "What am I going to do?"

"First thing to do is to pray and ask for forgiveness. It is crucial that you know that God is on your side. It is the only way to repair what is wrong in this situation. Remember that He worked to redeem sinners like us. God has not left you in this time of trouble, but you must seek him to find peace within yourself and to find strength so that you can take full responsibility for what has happened tonight. Can I pray with you right now?"

Jacob could only nod yes to the pastor, and they held hands while they took turns praying for forgiveness and strength.

When they were done praying the nurse brought Anthony and Chief Taylor into the room.

Pastor Maurice Smith greeted his members, then he turned to Jacob and said, "With your permission I would like to open the church. News of this tragedy is spreading throughout the community, and I feel that the congregation needs the word of God to put to rest the gossip and rumors that will split the church group. I believe that helping fellow Christians in this situation will give them something to do besides pointing fingers and placing blame."

Jacob could only nod in agreement with the Pastor. The pastor left the room after saying goodbye to Chief Taylor and Anthony.

Praying with the pastor gave Jacob a little more strength than he had felt since this situation began to unfold. Now he would draw on that strength to explain what had led to the night's painful conclusion.

He decided to start taking responsibility for the mess by explaining to Chief Taylor and Anthony what had happened.

The look of shock and dismay on Anthony's and Chief Taylor's faces were most intimidating to Jacob because he was used to most people looking at him with respect but these men wanted him to make sense of the nightmare that was still unfolding.

Anthony spoke first, "How are you feeling?"

In a deflated voice, the former chief answered, "Physically, unfortunately, I am doing well but mentally I am a wreck."

"As you know," said Chief Taylor, "I must ask you some sensitive questions."

"If you will, let me tell you what happened," Jacob suggested.

Both men nodded in agreement because it was far too awkward and uncomfortable to question a man of Jacob's integrity.

"After Wilma and I had eaten dinner, she fixed me a drink, and we were in the den talking about what had happened at your house today. Suddenly, I started to feel woozy. I told her that I wasn't feeling very well, and she said to me, 'Just let it happen, J. You see, I put poison in your food and this drink.'

"I dropped the glass and tried to get up, but I fell back on the couch. I asked, 'Wilma, why?' Then she turned into some person that I've never seen before. Her face took on a wicked look as she reached behind the couch and pulled out this bag of clothes and started to put them on. She said…"

"I have to right your wrong, honey. No one must know that you never loved me. I killed that bitch doctor you were going to leave me for, so maybe you might look at me the way you looked at her. But no, you just looked at me with sadness and then there were your bastard kids! You brought them into our home! I raised them and pretended that they were our children. Then Samantha, bless her little heart, came to me so I could help her trace her family tree through DNA testing."

"Then she laughed a hellish laugh and continued…"

"I couldn't let her do that-- find out that you are her real father so, she had to die, and I knew I'd get the one that looked like you, and acts so superior like you when I killed Sam. While you are dying just think about what I am doing to your precious daddy's little girl. Oh, I almost forgot, this outfit is for your dead brother. You know, the purple scarf for the Purple Heart the army gave him. These fatigues, I wore them when I killed Gail-Ann and Sam. Because of his army lies, you were able to live two lives. His lies gave you the right to humiliate me and the zombie face, well, that's because he's dead and I can't kill him so, it's in his image that I make this right."

"I pretended to be overcome by the poison and pass out.

Wilma kissed me and said, "I love you, J."

The deeply troubled man paused, then continued his recount of the nightmare everyone was living.

"I waited until the door closed and called the EMS but my main concern was finding Danielle. I had the hospital contact the department to track down Kevin because that's where I thought she would be, but Wilma got to her anyway. Have you heard anything about her condition? "

Both men were too stunned to respond right away. Finally, Anthony answered, "Danny is in guarded condition in ICU; she lost a lot of blood. She was stabbed in the upper shoulder twice, and she had glass in both feet. Slicks' condition has been upgraded to stable. He was stabbed in the stomach and somehow he managed to slow down the bleeding. He was shot in the arm, but it was a through and through so, he is going to be alright."

"What was Slicks doing there?" Jacob asked.

"He was still following Danny. He told us that he didn't think Danny was safe because Lindsey said 'This ain't over, bitch,' when she was arrested."

"I am glad he was there," Anthony said, shaking his head.

Chief Taylor continued to explain, "He explained to us that Samantha was helping him take a test to become a private investigator. I believed that he will make a good P. I." Chief Taylor said.

"Is Danny conscious?" Jacob asked hopefully.

"No, but being her next of kin, the doctors should be in here shortly to discuss her condition."

Anthony said, "Sir, I can't begin to understand this situation but know this, I will stand beside you while you work it out. I always have had and still have the greatest respect for you so, whatever I can do to make this easier just let me know."

"That goes for me as well, J. I am here for you. You can call me anytime, day or night. I will make time for you." Chief Taylor said as he extended his hand to Jacob.

Jacob looked into the face of his friend and knew that he meant what he said. He shook his hand and Anthony's too.

Jacob exhaled when the men left the room. Turning over in the hard hospital bed, he prayed for his soul and for the healing of his daughter.

CHAPTER SEVENTEEN

When Anthony called Lauren to bring some clothes to the hospital for Kevin, she became alarmed. Anthony tried to sooth her fears by telling her that everyone was alright, but he did not tell her about Slicks, Danny, Miss Wilma, or Chief J. He had a hard time digesting everything that had happened just in one day. Thinking back, he listed them, Sam's funeral, the attack on Danny and Lauren planned by Lindsey and a mad man, and now Miss Wilma killed almost everyone in Danny's family. How can anyone process this day? On the other hand, how can all this happen in one day? He hoped that he could explain it all to Lauren without her getting too upset and starting one of those painful headaches.

Well, he thought, 'if she does have one we are in the hospital.' He hoped to avoid adding her name to the list of family and friends who were already there.

As Lauren hurried through the hospital's parking lot carrying her husband's clothes that she knew would be too big for her brother, she knew something was wrong. She had reasoned it out on the ride uptown. If Kevin was here at University Hospital, then Danny was here, and if Anthony was there then there was a serious problem, but what she couldn't figure out is why Kevin needed dry clothes?

Anthony was waiting for her near the elevators and he looked like he had been through a terrible ordeal.

"Listen to me, Lauren," He said, taking her by the arm and leading her away from the ICU waiting room.

While Anthony was explaining the plight of their friends and family to his wife, across town Pastor Maurice Smith was in his office at the church putting the finishing touch on his sermon for tonight. Secretary, Clara Mayfield had sent out a recorded message for everyone to meet at the church for an emergency prayer meeting, and she had been screening phone calls from then on.

The Pastor was saying a prayer of strength and guidance when his secretary came into the office to inform him that the church was full of anxiously waiting members. Most of the confused members were wondering what this meeting was about because they had been at the church earlier attending the funeral for Samantha Johnston.

He walked to the pulpit with a heavy heart, but he knew the Lord would give him the words he needed tonight to comfort and lead his congregation. People filled with wonder and questions started taking their seats when they saw the minister.

"We are here tonight to pray for some members of our church that are in desperate need of our support. I want you to hear some information from me before rumors start to spread so, let me start." He said, wiping his glasses, which everyone knew was a stalling tactic used by the man to prepare them for bad news. "Danielle Johnston is in University Hospital's ICU." The crowd of people all gasped at the same time. Each of their faces mirrored the shock he was feeling, but he knew he must go on. "Sylvester Malone, known to most of you as Slicks is in critical condition, also at University Hospital, and Miss Wilma Johnston is deceased."

The members of the Lady Auxiliary Committee were crying, and moaning as other members were trying to console them.

Looking out at the members whispering to each other, the Pastor could tell that everyone wanted to know, what had happened?

"You will hear more about what happened through the news media and the justice system. But tonight I am here to urge you to do your duty as church people, and believers to support these families that have been torn apart by tragedy and destruction. Do not judge them, for if everyone's sins were made known, then all of us would fall short of being the Christians in which we portray ourselves. Again, I ask you not to judge for you are no better than these people who are in distress. It is only by the grace of God that you or your family are not, at this time, in a tragic situation."

The pastor paused for a second then went on, "We need to pray for the families, then we need to set up specific groups to meet the individual needs of our church members that are in crisis but first, we need to pray. I'm going to call the names of the members that are in need of our prayers and support. I know that they are not here so, I want one representative from this congregation to stand in their place."

"Sister Lindsey Williams."

Sister Anna-Marie Brown came forward to stand at the front of the church.

"Brother Sylvester Malone."

Deacon Donald Mayfield joined Sister Brown.

The Pastor's voice got heavy when he said, "Sister Danielle Johnston."

Everyone was surprised when Sister Teah Howard proudly walked to the front of the church and joined the others. Most people didn't think she had any initiative at all. Teah always seemed to need guidance in everything but tonight she was walking, almost arrogantly to stand in for Danielle.

Tears then fell from Reverend Smith's eyes as he called, "Sister Wilma Johnston."

With a heavy heart for her husband and best friend, Elise Smith joined the others at the front of the church to stand in for the late Wilma Johnston.

There was a lot of sniffling and crying as the pastor conditioned himself to continue.

Clearing his throat, he said, "Now I want the entire congregation to surround the people who are standing in for our fallen members."

"This is how it will look and feel to surround our troubled members with love. There is no big or little sin, for sin is why we go to church. To be forgiven for the things we have done that are not pleasing in the Lord's sight. For us to be forgiven by God, we must forgive others."

"Let us pray. Lord, we are asking for strength tonight. Give us strength to stand with and uphold these members of our church family. Unspeakable things have happened to them, and some of the members are fighting for their lives. Give us the strength to lift them, to carry them, to meet their needs and to give them comfort. We pray that Sister Wilma

Johnston is resting in peace." He started to sob. "She was a real believer and she tried to live her life in Your way, but she fell short. Please accept her into your kingdom and forgive her and all of us of our sins. Please do not let her good work be forever stained by what has driven her to these sinful acts.

Unable to continue he closed, "Please be present as we plan to encourage and be a lifeline to those that need You in a bad way. For it is in Your son Jesus' name we pray, Amen."

When he finished praying for everyone, the members began hugging and crying together and this went on for ten minutes.

After composing himself, the Pastor said, "Here is what I need to help the families in crisis. I need for the Missionary Society to meet with me in my office when I finish here. To further support our sisters and brothers that are in critical situations, the following committees will be created; a Counseling Committee that will focus on physical, sexual, gambling, and substance abuse. I need a prison board to bring the word to our sisters and brothers whom are in jail or incarcerated, a mental health committee, and a culinary committee to see that these families are fed, daily. You should make plans tonight and be ready to implement your plans tomorrow. Please meet as often as you can to make sure our programs are working. We ask God's blessing on our efforts."

Then he left the pulpit to get ready to meet with the Missionary group. It was time to put some real work into being a member of this group.

Meanwhile, Jacob was awakened from his fitful sleep by Danny's Dr. Nelson.

Laying her chart on the table, he said, "Mr. Johnston I have an update on Miss Johnston's condition." Jacob nodded a go-ahead nod at the tall, slender man.

She has two stab wounds on the shoulder. We have picked out all of the glass that was embedded in her feet and bandaged them. The biggest problem that we are facing is the amount of blood she has lost. To be honest with you sir, she nearly bled out. Right now, we are watching her hemoglobin levels to see if they stay steady, or she may need another blood transfusion."

"Is she suffering?" Jacob asked.

"We've given her medicine to manage her pain, but she's a fighter, she fought hard to stay awake but we need for her to rest and let her body heal. Right now, her condition is stable but guarded."

The word stable gave him a feeling of relief but the word guarded clinched his heart. He wouldn't feel at ease until he knew that Danny was out of danger.

Interrupting his thoughts the doctor added, "Does she have a living will?"

"Not that I am aware of,"

"Okay, we didn't get her properly registered when she arrived last night, and someone said that you were her legal guardian."

"I am her father," Jacob replied. For the first time, he could announce to the world that he was her father. If only Sam were here, he thought.

"Oh, that is even better." said the doctor. "Someone from intake will be in shortly to help you complete the forms. Is there anything else I can do for you?"

"Not that I can think of right now," Jacob answered extending his hand he said, "I want to thank you for saving my child."

"No problem," said the doctor as he left the room.

The next day evidence of the church's new committees was displayed. The culinary council supplied sandwiches and desserts in the waiting area, and one person from the church group stayed to serve and clean up.

While Danny slept another church member brought much needed personal hygiene products to Kevin, Anthony, Lauren, Ace, and Teah because they would not leave the hospital.

Later that night while Kevin was taking a shower, Slicks used his good shoulder to roll his wheelchair into Danny's room. Hearing the friction of the wheels on the tile floor, she woke when he entered the room.

Softly he said, "Hey, baby girl. How are you feeling?"

Barely speaking above a whisper, she said "Slicks," as her eyes filled with tears. When she looked at Slicks, she could still hear him screaming in agony. The realization came to her with a jolt that Slicks was almost killed trying to save her. Danny didn't think she would see him alive again.

"Don't cry, baby. Both of us survived and that is all that matters. Now, we need to get well. How do you feel?"

Swallowing hard she replied, "Like I've been run over by a truck, but I am glad to be feeling anything. Thank you, Slicks. Sam would be so proud."

Although he smiled, the pain of Sam's death still showed in his eyes, "Well, at least now I know I have a guardian angel looking out for me."

"For both of us," she added in a weak voice.

"Let me get out of here before my nurses and the deacon in my room find out I'm gone. Keep getting strong, Dan."

"I will," she answered as he rolled himself out of her room.

CHAPTER EIGHTEEN

Kevin came out of the bathroom feeling better after a good shower and shave. Looking over at Danny he was pleasantly surprised to see that Danny was looking at him.

"Dan? How do you feel?"

"I feel like every part of my body hurts, she answered. "My mouth is dry, can I have some water?"

Not being sure what she could have, he said, "First, let me call the nurse."

He grabbed her hand as he used the phone beside the bed to call the nurses' station. What he really wanted to do was to hug her and tell her how much he loved her, but as he looked at her he knew that would have to wait until she was much better because she looked so weak.

While the team of doctors and nurses examined her, he went to the waiting area to tell the others that she was awake.

Lauren said, "You should tell Chief J that she's awake."

Then all of a sudden fury swelled in his mind so powerful that it made his body rigid. Chief Jacob Johnston's actions almost cost him the woman that he loved. He couldn't even think about talking to him.

Everyone saw the change in Kevin's demeanor, but only Anthony spoke, "I'll tell him, after all, he is the only family she has, and he has the right to know."

Kevin didn't answer he just went to the window and looked at the people outside. He couldn't put his feelings into words all he knew was that he was very upset with the former Chief.

After eating a sandwich and chips left by a church member, he returned to Danny's room only to find that the Chief was visiting his daughter so, he went to visit Slicks.

Ace and Teah were in the room with him watching a program on the wall-mounted television. Everyone looked up when he came through the door.

After greeting everybody, he asked Slicks how he was doing.

"I'm going to be alright," Slicks said. "I've talked to Danny, and I feel that she will be alright, too. I'm so glad."

"How can I ever thank you for risking your life to save her?"

"There is no need to thank me, man. I wish I had been there for Sam."

"I know you will always love Sam, but you went way out for Danny, and I appreciate it."

"I was glad to do it, besides its good practice for us, right Ace?"

Ace nodded in agreement.

"Yeah, what's up?" Kevin asked the brothers.

"Sam left me a little money, and we are going into the private investigating business as soon as Ace passes the test."

"Wow! That's good news." Kevin said feeling very positive about their plans for the future.

"Chief Johnston said he would help us. With his experience, we are on our way!" Ace said.

Kevin's body seized again at the mention of the Chief's name.

Sitting up in his bed Slicks said, "No, no, no man! You can't hold what happened to Danny against him. He didn't hurt Danny and Sam, Miss Wilma did this!"

"Because of what the Chief did to her!"

"Miss Wilma had choices. Only she is responsible for her actions. She killed my Sam, and I hope she rots in hell."

"No!" Teah said. "We must forgive her, Pastor said so!"

"That's going to be hard for me." Slicks said. "You just remember, man, I am in the same boat as you, only my woman is dead." His voice broke, and a deep sob came from his soul. "You get a second chance. I don't." Pulling himself together he added, "Just think, the Chief is her father, and he is all she has left. I wouldn't rock that boat if I were you, you may lose."

"Slicks you can't get this upset, bro." Ace cut in, "Bring it down a notch."

"I am sorry. Please don't let me get you all worked up. I just want to thank you for looking out for Danny. I got to get back to her."

"Take care, man," Slicks said as Kevin hurried from the room.

He felt bad about getting Slicks in an agitated mood, and he hoped that he would calm down soon. There was so much going on that he had forgotten that Slicks was still mourning for Sam. He was right, Kevin thought, he did have a second chance with Danny.

He got to the room just in time to see Danny's newly found father kissing her and he felt the steam of resentment rising within his soul.

Seeing the tall man in hospital clothes made him seem less intimidating. So Kevin stared straight into the Chief's eyes and said, "Danny needs her rest. You need to try to come back later."

But that is where he made his biggest mistake because hospital clothes don't necessary make this man timid.

"You are confused, Kevin." The big man stated as he walked closer to Kevin. "You may need to come back later."

Not backing down Kevin asked, "Why is that?"

"Simple. You are not married to Danny, and I am her father. As such I can have you barred from this room. Do you really want to suffer that humiliation?"

Before he could answer Danny's weak voice broke in, "Dad, don't."

Both of them looked at her because even though she was half sleep she had called him Dad.

After a few seconds he said to Danny, "I won't, but Kevin and I are going to have a little talk." He looked over his shoulder at Danny and said, "I *will* be back in a minute." Then to Kevin, "Let's go to my room to discuss *your* future."

Kevin had so many emotions jumping around in his mind that he couldn't focus on just one. Walking to the Chief's room, he did remember what Slicks had said earlier. "He is her father, and he is all she has left. I wouldn't rock that boat, you may lose."

Once Chief Johnston was in his room, he turned to face Kevin. "What's your problem with me?"

Choosing his words carefully he said, "I am upset with you for almost getting Danny killed. It is entirely your fault that she is in a hospital bed fighting for her life."

"Really?" The chief responded. "I could be upset with you for the same thing. Isn't your *wife* sitting in jail because she tried to kill Danny and your sister? And if we hadn't gotten there in time they both would have been raped by your *wife's* uncle. I won't even compare notes with you about your affair with Lindsey while dating my daughter."

The realization of the truth hit him like cold water being splashed in his face. This had been a very long day, and he had forgotten everything that happened earlier because he almost lost Danny.

"Take a moment and think about it." Chief Jacob said staring into the eyes of his future son-in-law.

After several moments, Kevin said, "I guess we are in the same situation. We both put her in danger."

"I would say so. Danny has been living in double triangles for a long time, and it has been rough on her. She needs to be able to recover without having to think about us being at odds with each other. I'd like it if we could work together without causing her more stress."

Kevin just nodded.

"She is going to need a lot of support when she is released from the hospital both physically and mentally. One of the things she will not worry about is you and me. Do you agree?"

Kevin said, "Yes I do."

He wanted to resist but how could he hold a grudge against this man when his own actions nearly got Danny and Lauren hurt or killed.

The Chief continued, "All three houses will be sources of pain for her so, I will have to rent a place for her to convalesce."

"She could stay with Anthony and Lauren. There are contractors at their house as we speak. They are tearing out the kitchen to completely rebuild it. It should be finished in a couple of days."

"That is good because I just made arrangements to sell my house. I really can't live there anymore, and I know that Danny couldn't find any peace there either." The Chief explained.

The atmosphere became more relaxed as both men sat down to make plans for Danny.

"Ace approached me about buying the cabin for him and Teah," Kevin explained. "That's fine with me because I could never go back there to live so, I'll be living with Anthony and Lauren until Danny is well and I see what she plans to do."

Right at that moment the doctor entered the room to give a report on Danny's condition. Realizing what position he was in, Kevin asked humbly if he could be included in the briefing, and graciously the Chief conceded.

A week later, Danny was released from the hospital with a heavy schedule of outpatient physical therapy. Her father took her to these sessions because everyone else had returned to work. The Chief was pleased to do this with her so he could be with her as her father before she married Kevin. The couple hadn't announced their plans, but Jacob knew that if Kevin loved Danny as much as he had loved Gail-Ann, then it was just a matter of time before he would ask Danny to marry him.

Later that week, Chief Johnston planned a small private graveside service for Wilma because she wouldn't want a big public display after all that happened. Some people would really mourn her death, but more people would just want to gossip about her fall from grace.

At 10 o'clock that Thursday morning, Jacob drove himself to the burial area for his wife of thirty years. It was hard for him to walk toward her waiting grave knowing that he alone was responsible for her lying in that expensive casket. Jacob wished he could have done things better but never would he regret loving Gail-Ann.

Jacob hadn't let anyone know about this service because he felt this was something he had to do alone. However, he was shocked when he walked over the hill to the grave site to see that there were chairs, and people were in them. At first, J thought he was in the wrong place, but then he recognized the Ladies' Auxiliary that Wilma belonged to and then he saw Anthony, Lauren, Slicks, Ace, Wes, Chief Taylor, and Kevin who stood as he approached. Tears started falling from Jacob's eyes for he didn't think he deserved this outpouring of support. He shook hands with all of them and thanked them for coming and when he got to Kevin, he saw Danny.

Seeing her at the funeral of the woman who both raised her, and tried to kill her caused him to lose complete control. He hugged her and cried out loud for her and Wilma to forgive him.

The women of the auxiliary comforted both of them and a protective Kevin helped Danny to her seat while a hovering Lauren was instantly by her side.

The service was short and meaningful as Pastor Smith reminded every one of the love and life of Wilma Johnston. He urged them to not let the spiritual weakness of Mrs. Johnston overshadow all of the good things she had done for the people who were present for her going home, as well as others.

When the service was over, Lauren invited everyone to her house for lunch, in her newly rebuilt kitchen, and it was sponsored by the Ephesians Baptist Church Ladies Auxiliary. Jacob went to Wilma's casket and asked her to forgive him. While he was saying goodbye to Wilma, he asked her to send him a sign if she forgave him. When Jacob turned toward Danny, a white dove flew between them. He took that as her answer from beyond the grave.

Everyone had parked their cars on the other side of the graveyard, so Ace walked back with Jacob to his vehicle. He turned around when he heard a car motor behind them. It was Kevin driving Ace's Jeep Grand Cherokee into the graveyard's access road to get Danny. Smiling he said to Ace, "That boy is going to make a great son-in-law."

But Ace was anxious to talk to the former Chief about the detective agency that he and his brother Slicks were starting.

Pulling out of the graveyard he asked Ace, "What kind of name is B and K Detective Service?"

"I am afraid that Slicks won't even talk about changing the name because it was named after Samantha."

Frowning he asked, "Samantha? I would think he would call it Sam Spade."

Laughing, Ace said, "No Chief J, it's for Baby Cakes. Wes and I finally convinced him that no one would hire us with the name Baby Cakes so, Teah came up with B. and K. She said it sounded mysterious and he agreed."

"I get it now. Slicks really loved Samantha, didn't he?"

"He'll have regrets the rest of his life because he wouldn't give up the streets for her. But I'm not making that mistake, because when the business starts going well I'm going to marry Teah."

"That is the right thing to do. Never let anything keep you from the one you love, especially if that person loves you back."

"Think you'll find that kind of love again?" Ace asked.

"I can't even reflect on that yet. I am just grateful for what I have now."

CHAPTER NINETEEN

The old saying, "What doesn't kill you will make you stronger" was true, Jacob thought as he watched the girls, Lauren, Teah, and the Ladies Auxiliary prepare for Danny and Kevin's wedding. He felt so proud when Kevin came to ask him for permission to marry Danny.

They both had laughed when the Chief said, "I must do my fatherly duty to tell you that if you hurt her, I will mess you up."

Sitting there laughing, they both knew that the former Chief was not playing. Although a part of him knew that he didn't deserve this joy. Jacob would put that doubt aside and play the part of the father-in-law-to-be.

In late July, Chief J found himself standing in the church's vestibule with Anthony and Kevin waiting for the signal that the wedding was starting. He had so many emotions when the usher came to take him to his daughter. He wished that her mother could be here, and that thought made him think about Sam, and then he thought about Wilma. She would have had everything organized and ready to go. Well, he sighed, "I'll have to be happy enough for all of them."

The usher lead him to a choir room where he saw Danny dressed in the loveliest wedding gown he'd ever seen. She looked just like her mother, and this brought tears to his eyes.

Going over to her he said, "You look beautiful!"

He hugged her and wanted to have a meltdown, but she wouldn't understand so instead, he released her.

Looking at her he said, "I must do this as my fatherly duty so here it goes, Danny, are you sure you want to marry Kevin?"

Looking serious she answered, "Dad, I've loved him for a very long time. I've loved him when I didn't want to. I am very sure this is the man I want to spend the rest of my life with."

He kissed her on the nose as he had done all of her life, and said, "Let's not keep the man waiting."

"I love you, Dad," Danny said, giving him a quick hug.

"I love you, too."

The doors to the vestibule opened then Jacob and his beautiful daughter, Danny started down the aisle. Everyone stood and gave a collective ah, to express their appreciation of the stunning bride as she walked on the rose print aisle runner toward the man of her dreams.

Before a packed church, Pastor Smith prayed for the couple, then he announced that the couple would light candles for the family members who have passed on so, Danny walked to one side of the room, and Teah said, "Danielle is lighting the first candle for her mother Gail-Ann Johnston, and the second one for Wilma Johnston." As Kevin walked to the other side of the room, Slicks took the mic and said, "Kevin is lighting a candle for Samantha Johnston. May they all rest in peace."

There wasn't a dry eye in the church because most of the people attending the wedding knew the difficulties this family had experienced. After a moment, Pastor Smith continued with the service.

"Who presents this woman to be married to this man?"

With great pride and thankfulness, Jacob said, "I do."

Kevin mouthed, "Thank you."

Then he took his seat feeling a sense of peace, a feeling he hadn't felt in a long time. Then he thought of what Wilma would say at a time like this, it would have been a verse from the Bible, Psalm 30:5, "Weeping may endure for a night, but joy comes in the morning."

98312379R00134

Made in the USA
Columbia, SC
23 June 2018